Ride the Man Down

RIDE THE MAN DOWN
Luke Short

Thorndike Press
Thorndike, Maine

Library of Congress Cataloging in Publication Data:

Short, Luke, 1908-1975.
 Ride the man down.
  Reprint. Originally published: Garden City
N.Y.: Doubleday, Doran, 1942.
 1. Large type books. I. Title.
[PS3513.L68158R5 1981]   813'.54   81-4809
ISBN 0-89621-277-7   AACR2

All rights reserved.
Copyright © 1942 by Frederick Glidden.
Copyright renewed 1969 by Frederick Glidden.
This book may not be reproduced in whole or in part, by mimeograph or any other means, without permission. For information address: Bantam Books, Inc.

Large Print edition available through arrangement with H. N. Swanson, Inc., and Florence Glidden.

Set in 16/18 Plantin by Duarte Typesetting Lewiston, Maine

Cover design by Marc Rosenthal

Ride the Man Down

Chapter 1

The train passed the stock pens, and when it was even with the station Will Ballard slung his saddle out into the night. Afterward he swung down from the bottom step of the caboose onto the cinder apron, breaking his speed by digging in his heels so that he came to a halt some twenty feet from the station platform. He stood there, hands on hips, a big man in work-soft waist overalls and scuffed half boots, and looked toward the station platform.

Russ Schultz, who had got off the front of the caboose, broke his run on the platform and came to a stop in front of the agent, and the two of them watched the red and green lights of the caboose recede into the chill spring darkness.

Schultz said something to the agent then and started for the corner of the station nearest Will, and Will walked toward him.

The dry crunch of cinders caused Schultz to look up, and when he saw Will he halted abruptly. Will mounted the platform and came toward him and said mildly, "Think I'd let you see him alone, Russ?"

Schultz said sullenly, "Damn you, no. I didn't," and brushed past him, turning the corner of the station and heading toward the town, and Will tramped down the platform. To the agent he said, "Evening, Earl," and halted in the patch of faint light cast through the soot-stained bow windows of the station. Stooping a little, he peered inside at the agent's clock. The lamplight touched his face briefly, revealing a weariness that was physical and only of the moment. It was a long face, its sharp jaw line blurred faintly by dark beard stubble, its thick hooding eyebrows powdered faintly with dust, the whole shape of it angular and faintly truculent now.

He straightened and the agent said, "Russ says you ain't quite through, Will."

"That's right," Will said pleasantly. His voice was courteous, easy, and held a distinct suggestion that the agent mind his own business. He nodded, again pleasantly, and retraced his steps as far as his saddle back in the dark. Picking it up, he held it by the horn and slung it over his shoulder and then tramped beyond the station toward the town.

Boundary's main street started behind the station, a wide sweep of pock-marked dust between the ragged double line of store fronts. The night wind off the flats stirred up an occasional eddy of dust that marched drunkenly across the squares of light laid out by the store lamps and spent itself under the galleried porch of the hotel at the four corners. It was a chill wind, token of snows still unmelted in the Indigos, and it gave Will an awareness of spring and, for himself, of a coming trouble, and he hurried.

For Will Ballard had sat passive through a whole winter and on into the spring calf branding, and now he was in a hurry.

He tramped the uncertain planking of the walk as far as the Belle Fourche Saloon across from the Stockman's House and mounted the steps and shouldered his way through the swing doors. Pausing just inside them, he scowled against the sudden brightness of the overhead lamps and let his saddle slide from his shoulder to the floor. Most of the country was still at the calf branding he had left this morning, so that the saloon was doing a slack business, but a single careful glance told him the right men were here, and he moved on forward. He said, "How are you, Harve?" to Garretson standing at the bar and passed him, having no business with him, and nodded to one of the house men playing Canfield at an idle keno table.

The table in the rear held his attention, for Schultz stood beside it, beside Joe Kneen, too, who sat at it. The two other men seated there—a drummer of some kind and Ray Cavanaugh—he noted and forgot before he halted across from Schultz.

Will looked mildly at Joe Kneen and said, "How do you like his story, Joe?" in his pleasant, quiet voice.

Kneen kept on riffling a pack of cards while he glanced up at Will. He was a man past middle age, heavy-boned and lean, dressed in a clean black suit, and his way of moving was purposely unhurried. In half a lifetime of petty officialdom supplemented by successful gambling Sheriff Kneen had cultivated a bland, pale-eyed, and unblinking stare that was calculated either to disconcert or anger a man. It did neither to Will now, as Kneen knew it would not, and he turned his head to look at Schultz.

"You got a story, Russ?"

Schultz said blandly, "Me? No," and he was watching Will, almost smiling at him. Ray Cavanaugh snickered, and Will looked down at him briefly, blankly, and then returned his gaze to Schultz. The man's broad, surly face was oddly swollen around the right cheekbone, which held a small cut too.

"Well, well," Will murmured, and now he regarded Joe Kneen with a kind of speculative insolence in his green eyes. He put both hands on the table now and leaned forward and said mildly, "Joe, don't fill out any warrant for me. I'll tear it up."

He and Kneen regarded each other for long seconds, and Will came slowly erect.

Kneen said, "What warrant?"

"Ask Russ."

Kneen said to Schultz, "What warrant?"

"What's he talkin' about?" Schultz asked, almost smiling again. Once more Ray Cavanaugh snickered, and this time Will looked at him steadily, his eyes bland and hard. Cavanaugh was a wry-faced Irishman, small, dressed in shabby range clothes that were not clean. Will saw a bright malice in his face now and he said softly, "Get out of here, Ray."

In the thin silence now the drummer got up from the table and left it, and nobody noticed his departure. Cavanaugh regarded Will carefully, his smile fading slowly. He glanced hopefully at Kneen and found only a neutrality there. He sat a moment longer, with a fading defiance, and then he rose. Will saw him look at Schultz, a fleeting question in his eyes, and then he turned and strolled unconcernedly away from the table.

Kneen said quietly, patiently, to Will, "What warrant?"

"Any warrant, Joe. Any warrant," Will murmured.

Kneen sat more erect now, and a faint anger edged into his voice as he said flatly, "I want to know."

Will tilted his head toward Schultz but did not look at him and said meagerly to Kneen, "Russ claimed a calf in this morning's gather and we argued. I hit him, and he left to swear out a warrant for theft."

Kneen said, "Bide's roundup boss. What did he say?"

Will said dryly, mildly, "Why, Bide was

out on another gather. That's kind of a handy place to be when his own foreman has a row. Russ didn't wait for him."

Both Will and Kneen glanced at Schultz now and saw the faint smile on his face. Kneen said with rising irritability, "Well, Russ?"

"Nothin'," Schultz said blandly. "Nothin'."

Will nodded and said mildly to Kneen, "Just remember, Joe. No warrant," and started to go.

Kneen said sharply, "Will!"

Will halted by Kneen's elbow and looked down at him, and Kneen said carefully, "Hatchet never was so big it could tell me what to do. Not even when Phil Evarts was alive. So be careful."

Will smiled faintly, watching the anger in Kneen's eyes. "I'm careful, Joe," he murmured. "Just so you are." He glanced briefly at Schultz and then again at Kneen and said, "Just be sure that Hatchet's dead before you and Bide and all the others dig a grave for it."

"Phil Evarts is dead, and Phil Evarts was Hatchet," Kneen said softly. "You don't make big tracks any more, Will. Just remember it."

Will was utterly motionless as Kneen ceased talking, and his weather-browned face altered slightly, settling into an expression of amusement. "Why, Joe," he drawled, "you're too old to be called a liar. But I'll prove you one."

"I'll worry about that," Kneen said sardonically.

"I think you will," Will said, and he turned and tramped forward toward the door, where he picked up his saddle and went out.

Out in the night he paused on the plank walk a moment. Something was queer in all this. Schultz had backed down, and that was not like Schultz or like Bide Marriner. A sudden impatience was on him now, and he left the walk and cut across the street, his pace hurried. He passed a single lighted store and he slowed a little, looking inside. He could not see Lottie, although her father was at his desk in the balcony over the rear half of the store.

He went on, and at the end of the block the stores ended and he was in the residence part of Boundary. At the second house from the corner, a small frame affair behind a new painted fence, he turned in at the gate and skirted the house. Halted by the back door, he knocked softly and then turned his back to it, breathing deeply of the night air. He was aware now of a sudden iron ache in his legs, token of ten days of constant riding.

At the sound of the door opening he turned, lifting off his Stetson, and said gently to the girl standing in the door holding the lamp, "I'm taking your mare, Lottie."

"I'll get a lantern, Will," Lottie Priest said.

Will waited, hearing her move in the kitchen, and he felt a slow stirring of pleasure. There was something in the quiet way this girl accepted things, calmly and without question, that had been a tonic to his restlessness these last months.

When she stepped out with the lantern and closed the door behind her Will did not move for a second. He looked long at her, until his searching, almost hungry gaze provoked a smile from her. She was a tall girl, dressed almost demurely in a dark suit that the town demanded of its schoolteacher. Her face was almost oval, with full lips, a straight, small nose, and quick, eager eyes that were almost the golden color of her hair. Will knew she was wondering why he had left the calf branding and that she would not ask until he told her.

As they turned toward the barn she said with gentle derision, "It couldn't have been poker, where you lost your horse, Will. You've still got your saddle."

Will said, "I think this thing is going to break, Lottie," and he saw Lottie's swift look of apprehension. He paused to open the door of the barn, and Lottie stepped inside. Will walked over to the corner where the chestnut mare was stalled and stroked her silken rump, murmuring to her. Lottie hung the lantern on a nail beside the stall upright, and then Will looked at her. They held each other's gaze a long, troubled moment, and Lottie said quietly, "When, Will?"

"I thought it was this morning," Will said, and he told her of the quarrel with Schultz. She listened to his brief account of everything that had passed in the saloon. As he finished he lifted the blanket off the stall partition and threw it over the mare's back.

"What does it mean, Will?" Lottie asked.

Will turned his head to look at her. "Bide's ready to start. He wanted to see if I'd take it from Schultz."

"And Joe Kneen's against you too?" Lottie said quietly.

Will nodded. His green eyes were brash, lighted with a recklessness she could not help but observe. "Seventy thousand empty acres of Hatchet range is real loot, Lottie. A sheriff's star doesn't change a man's greed."

He lifted the saddle on now and cinched it tightly. Lottie leaned against the stall post, arms folded across her breasts, and watched his swift, sure movements, the sudden coil of his back muscles under his calico shirt as he yanked the cinch. When he was finished he rubbed his hand over his face, and the passage of his palm down his beard-stubbled cheek made a faint rasping sound in the silence.

This gesture of weariness stirred the girl to speech, and she said calmly, "I suppose the pack had to gather sometime, now the old wolf is dead. You knew they would, Will."

Will said musingly, softly, "If old Phil was still alive we'd be hunting Bide Marriner out of the country tonight. Joe Kneen, too, sheriff or not."

"But he isn't alive," Lottie said quietly.

"And it's just the other way. They'll be hunting you."

Will's smile was slow, tolerant. "If you worked for Phil Evarts you expected that."

"But you're not working for Phil now—you're working for his brother," Lottie said swiftly, almost sharply.

Will said gently, "It's still Hatchet."

"A different Hatchet," Lottie insisted. She stepped away from the post now and came up to him and put a hand on his arm.

"Will, listen to me," she said. "Everybody knows John Evarts doesn't want to hold out. He can't. Everyone knows it but you—and Phil's daughter. But you're still blind—and you make the whole country angry, like you did Ray Cavanaugh tonight. Will, let Hatchet go! Let them take it! You can't prop it up alone! Let it go!"

"It's still Hatchet," Will repeated stubbornly.

Lottie smiled then, a troubled smile of mild despair and defeat. "I tried, Will, but I guess you're blind to me too." She shrugged. "It's whatever you say." She paused and repeated softly, looking at him, "It always has been whatever you say, Will. You know that."

Will covered her hand with his and then gathered up the reins and led the mare out into the night. He stepped into the saddle and looked down at her. The light from the lantern still inside the barn made a faint aura of gold of Lottie's hair.

She looked up at him, smiling. "I teach this town's children, Will, but it doesn't own me. Just remember that when you need me."

"I'll remember. Good night, Lottie."

Will kneed the mare around to start down the alley, but he checked her immediately and looked down at the girl.

"Lottie," he said in a troubled voice, "don't talk that way again. I've got to know I'm right."

Lottie was silent a long moment and then she said gently, "It's whatever you say, Will."

Will came really awake only when the chestnut mare halted by the corral trough at Hatchet sometime after midnight.

He stepped stiffly out of the saddle, chilled and aching, and, out of long habit, looked over at the house bulking long and low under the piled-up blackness of its surrounding cottonwoods. There was a lamp lighted in the office, and at sight of it his sleepy mind roused. He stared at it a moment, a faint apprehension taking hold of him.

Quickly, then, he turned his mare into the corral and started for the house. He came abreast of the log cookshack and bunkhouse and was past it when someone called softly from the bunkhouse, "Will."

He hauled up, recognizing the voice of Ike Adams. He had left orders for Ike to stay at calf branding this morning, and he was here now. Will started for the black doorway when Ike came out and came up to him and halted in the darkness.

"Bide moved the wagon over to Russian Springs after you left," Ike said in his taciturn voice.

Will was quiet a long moment, and then he said softly, "So." He knew now why Schultz had picked the quarrel this morning. Schultz had made his threat and caught the stock train, knowing Will would follow him for a showdown with Kneen. And Bide, having pulled Will out of the way, through Schultz, moved the roundup wagon to Russian Springs. A feeling of anger and a kind of sheepish guilt was hot in him now, and he shifted his feet faintly in the dark. Ike said, "They're waitin' for you up at the house. Danfelser too."

"All right, Ike," Will said and turned again toward the house.

As he approached the near wing of the dark building he saw the door open and Sam Danfelser move into its frame. The shape of him was big and blocky in the doorway, and a quick disappointment that Will could not analyze came over him and was gone immediately. This was the man Celia Evarts was going to marry, the man that dead Phil Evarts had approved for his daughter. Hatchet would be his someday, and he had every right to be here, and it occurred to Will now that his own weariness had made him impatient. As he came up he said, "How are you, Sam?"

Danfelser did not answer. He stepped aside, and Will got a brief glimpse of his square face, of the troubled, surly alertness there. He was a young man with a full-jawed, wind-ruddied face topped by short-cut hair as bleached as new rope. Not so tall as Will, he was heavier, thicker across the chest, and when he stepped back out of the door there was a hint of tremendous stubborn strength in his movements.

Will stepped into the office now, pulling off his Stetson, and nodded to Hatchet's owner, John Evarts, who was sitting on the worn leather sofa. Will moved across the room, hearing Sam close the door behind him, and pitched his hat on the rickety rolltop desk in the corner. He heard Celia Evarts coming down the corridor that led onto the rest of the house and he glanced up, his back still to Evarts and Danfelser.

Celia Evarts came in, then, tying the belt of her maroon wrapper, and when she saw Will she smiled. Will's answering grin was easy, friendly, and it came fleetingly to him again that in this girl he was seeing a pleasant and lovely joke of nature. For she had been sired by a man who was big and black and ugly and whose eyes windowed the tough, reckless spirit of him, a spirit without mercy and with only meager friendliness. Yet in this girl Phil Evarts' bony ugliness had been refined into a thin-faced, slim loveliness with hair like her father's falling thick and curling to her shoulders. She was small, and her eyes were Phil's—as gray and reckless, but with an open friendliness in him. She was Phil

Evarts, blood and soul, but with the dross gone.

She stepped just into the room and put her shoulders against the wall, and Will turned and said mildly, "Ike told me," and sat on the desk.

John Evarts said diffidently, "Well, it may not mean anything, you know."

Sam moved away from the door and said heavily, without looking at Will, "That was a simple trick to fall for, Will."

"Wasn't it?" Will agreed.

He was watching Evarts now, noting that he had pulled on trousers and coat over his nightshirt. He was a kindly-seeming man with a mussed ruff of gray hair over a face mellowed by small triumphs in small ambitions. He was the owner of Hatchet now, named so by his brother who had so little faith in the shrewdness of women that he had put his ranch in the hands of a man without any shrewdness at all. The irony of it was never more apparent than now, Will thought, and he did not speak.

Evarts said sleepily, "I think Ike is being spooked. Bide's roundup boss. He can order the wagon wherever he wants."

He looked at Will and Will was stubbornly

silent, and Evarts crossed his legs with a kind of irritability in the movement.

"You can't keep a roundup crew off your range," he went on, almost pleading. "It probably doesn't mean a thing."

Will murmured softly, flatly, "He'll stay there," and saw the distress mount in John Evart's eyes. He had seen it there before, when John Evarts had to make a decision and refused to. He would refuse this one, just as he had refused to face each crisis since Phil Evarts' death. And the long list of these was graven in Will's memory as irrevocably as epitaphs on gravestones, for Will had pictured them thus—each as a new death for Hatchet.

It had begun with the blizzards in February which piled foot after foot of snow upon the flats until Phil Evarts, helpless and raging, had ridden out to his death in the storm in a vain attempt to cut the drift fences. That nightmare week had wiped out all but a remnant of Hatchet's cattle, leaving them piled in frozen windrows against the drift fences. Phil's death had set in motion the chain of events that brought John Evarts to Hatchet as owner. The crises began then and followed each other with the regularity of beads on a string. John Evarts could not swing loans from the bank, and the Hatchet crew, with no loyalty for a man who would not provide for them, broke up and drifted away with their wages owing. So now Hatchet's vast range that Phil Evarts had plundered from weaker men was empty and stood waiting for a man strong enough to take it. And that man, everyone knew, was Bide Marriner. In the struggle for more range and more water holes for more cattle that made up the life of a big rancher, Phil Evarts had outguessed and outfought Bide Marriner at every turn. But Phil was dead and Bide was alive, the ultimate crisis that John Evarts must face.

Will had known the showdown would come after the snows. Phil Evarts had been a brigand, tougher than his tough neighbors, but his brother was a reasonable man, which in this country was interpreted as a sign of weakness. So now these outfits, large and small, were closing in on him and forcing his hand, for there was nothing between them and the empty limitless ranges of Hatchet except a timid aging man and an unpaid skeleton crew, of which Will was boss. A dozen times Will had decided to drift, and each time he had stayed, hating himself, helpless, waiting for the inevitable.

And now it was here. Bide had moved onto Hatchet under cover of calf burning, and John Evarts didn't want to see it. It was in his face and Will watched it, just as Sam and Celia were watching it.

John said reluctantly then, "Maybe you're right, Will. But Bide might lease it from us."

Sam Danfelser said flatly, "That's not the way to handle Bide, John."

His heavy positive voice seemed to wipe out John Evarts' words; it was more than a contradiction, and the older man strangely seemed to welcome it.

Sam put his big hands on the back of the chair in front of him and spoke slowly now to Evarts.

"Bide won't lease. Phil took Russian Springs away from him, and he figures it's his. He won't pay for it."

"What would satisfy him?" Evarts asked.

Sam said flatly, positively, "Give it to him. He's leading the pack. Cut the ground from under him and you've got them beat. Give it to him."

Will made no move, said nothing, but he

watched Celia. He could see the protest mount in her eyes, and he knew Sam Danfelser saw it, too, and didn't care.

Celia said challengingly, "If Bide wanted a chunk of D Cross would you give it to him, Sam?"

Sam regarded her coolly, almost impersonally, and nodded. "If I'd stolen it from him and didn't have a crew to fight for it, yes. I'd give it back before he took it—and a lot more."

Celia looked to John Evarts now, silently appealing to him. And Sam was watching him, too, just as silently forcing his will upon him. Under the scrutiny of them, Evarts was uncomfortable, but some decision was necessary and he knew it. He sighed and said, "I believe you're right, Sam. He'll take it anyway."

"Give it to him before he takes it," Sam said. He was pleased with himself, and he could not keep a smugness entirely from his voice.

Celia looked fleetingly at Will, who was rubbing the edge of the boot-scarred desk, watching his hand, completely quiet, out of this. He was not going to help her.

She turned from him to her uncle, then,

spoke with bitter resignation. "Give Russian Springs to Bide, John, and you'll have every outfit begging on our doorstep."

Sam said easily, confidently, "Bide's the only one to worry about. The rest will sing small when he's satisfied."

Again Celia looked at Will, and again he was not watching this. She spoke almost with desperation. "You pay Will to run Hatchet, John. Ask him."

Sam shuttled his glance to Will and spoke immediately, aggressively. "John knows what Will would say. He doesn't agree with it."

John Evarts looked relieved at Sam's words, as if Sam had saved him from saying the same thing. Now he said, "We'll ride over to Russian Springs early, Will. I'll talk to Bide myself."

"All right," Will said mildly.

Sam turned toward the door then, and John Evarts, saying good night, went past Celia into the other part of the house.

Sam paused by the door, his hand on the knob, and said, "I'll sleep here, Celia. Coming, Will?"

"I've got a little work yet."

Sam looked at Celia then, and his

stubborn face softened a little. "Good night, Celia."

"Good night, Sam."

Will toed the rickety swivel chair up to the desk and sat down heavily. He reached down the red-covered talley book from a desk pigeonhole and poked among the papers until he found the stub of a pencil. He knew Celia had not left the room, but he did not look at her.

She came over to the desk then and shoved the papers aside and sat on the desk top beside him. Will glanced up and saw her watching him, and because he knew she wanted to talk and that there was no use trying to hide anything from her, he pitched the pencil back among the papers and tilted back in his chair. His black hair lay awry on his forehead, and he did not brush it back.

Celia mumured with a kind of self-derision, "It's been a long time since I was spanked and sent to bed this way."

"Me too," Will said and grinned. He thought of Schultz and he murmured, "I deserved mine, I reckon."

They were silent for a while, each lost in the still private labyrinth of thought. Celia said finally, "Sam's so sure," in a small, doubting voice and looked questioningly at Will.

He didn't answer her, because he knew she didn't want him to. "What will Bide do?" she asked then.

"Take Hatchet. All of it."

Celia didn't speak, and Will went on in a low, hard voice, "Bide's hungry, and all the lickings Phil gave him didn't cure it. He'll be hungry until he gets Hatchet."

"Sam doesn't think so."

"No," Will said quietly, "I know he doesn't." He glanced at Celia, and for a long moment they looked in each other's eyes, and then Celia looked away. Will didn't have to apologize to her: she knew and she agreed with him.

Again they were silent, and Will felt his weariness settle on him, but oddly he was resigned and at peace. The full sum of John Evarts' weakness was known to him now, and that knowledge was some comfort. He knew Celia felt it, too, and he reflected idly upon that. There were times, like now, when he could tell what this girl was thinking, and there was no need for speech between them. During these six years he had been with Hatchet he had seen her grow from girlhood into womanhood and pledge herself to marry Sam Danfelser, and yet he was certain he understood her better than Sam ever would. He understood her better than he did Lottie he reflected, and it was Lottie he would marry someday.

He heard Celia sigh now, the sound of it small, almost inaudible, and he stirred restlessly in his chair and murmured, "We're a couple of mavericks, kid."

Celia nodded soberly, her eyes grave. "Why have you stuck, Will?" she asked gently.

"I don't know. Habit, I reckon." He scowled and looked up at her. "Why have you? Sam wants to take you away from Hatchet."

"But not until he's clear of debt," Celia said. There was a suggestion of resentment in her tone that Will ignored, knowing she was still smarting from Sam's overbearing advice.

"That's sound," he conceded.

Celia was silent a moment, and then she sighed. "Poor Will," she said softly.

Will looked sharply at her, scowling, and she went on: "You've been top dog too long to like this, haven't you?"

Will stirred restlessly under her gaze, and suddenly his lean face broke into a wry smile. "All right, I have. But those days are gone."

"Are they, Will?" She was looking at him intently, as if his reply would also answer some deep unsolved question within her.

Will said almost harshly, "John Evarts says so. I work for him."

Celia slid off the desk now, and she was still watching him gravely. "I don't believe you," she said simply. "You don't believe it yourself, either. Good night, Will."

Chapter 2

Will came awake next morning with the instant realization that he had overslept. It was a gray day, and one of the bunkhouse windows was banging noisily in the wind. Still half drugged with sleep, he rose and saw that Sam Danfelser's blankets were empty.

He shut the window and pulled on his boots. Washing hurriedly, he stepped out of the bunkhouse and glanced toward the house. It was a single-story affair of stone with timber wings and had a high veranda running its length under cottonwoods that were barely leafed now. There were no horses at the tie rail between the two trees in front of the veranda, and he wheeled and poked his head into the cookshack adjoining the bunkhouse. Of the five places set at one of the long plank tables, three were empty.

He stood for a moment, his mind slow to

accept this. Evarts and Sam and Ike had breakfasted early and ridden out, Ike doubtless on ranch business. But Sam and John had set out for Russian Springs without him. Moreover, they must have warned the cook and Ike against waking him.

He tramped back into the bunkhouse, gathered up his jumper and hat and shell belt, and headed for the corral. Lottie's mare had been turned out to pasture with the other horses, but she was gentle and he caught her easily. Will's anger was edging him now, for it was a universal rule that the horses were never turned out until everyone had a mount. Evarts had left plenty of evidence that he didn't want him along, and this realization touched a stubborn streak in Will.

Once mounted, he cut east from the ranch, letting Lottie's mare run off her spirits until she settled down to an alternate walk and lope. Evarts and Sam had clung to the old wagon road which was level riding to Russian Springs. Will kept a little north, heading across country, and was soon in the bare hills behind Hatchet.

From this mild elevation the greening new

grass lay stretched before him on all sides, broken now and then by the darker patches of timber and small growth along the watercourses. As far as he could see now, this range was empty, and Will was reminded again of the terrible winter past. Where he was riding now there had been four feet of snow. Off to the west, behind him, the the pine-clad Indigos shouldering blackly into the gray sky and dividing this Basin from the Indian reservation to the west, had not proved a barrier for those storms. They had come in over Indian Ridge to the north, so that Will, even now, regarded the Ridge with a deep malevolence. It lay in sight of these hills here, a high, bleak, timber-and-canyon-snarled badlands whose deep reaches stretched from the Indigos to the lower Salt Hills to the distant east. A footless lot of small ranchers fought for a bare living there where Phil Evarts had pushed them. Indian Ridge joined the Indigos and the Salt Hills, like the bar in the letter *H*, and it was below this bar that Hatchet cattle had died by the hundreds, so that Will this morning was rarely out of sight of a bleaching skeleton.

He kept east and a little north, and after

midday dropped down a bald slope past one of Hatchet's line shacks and later picked up the road. This shack, Will knew, was Phil Evarts' first home in this country, his original homstead. He had been settled here only months before he started reaching out to the west. To the east was a waterless stretch, relieved only by Russian Springs, and Phil had not bothered with that until later. Then he had seized it from Bide Marriner, and now Bide had it back—given to him by John Evarts. Will thought of that darkly, impatience edging him now.

An hour later Will saw two horsemen ahead of him, and he lifted his horse into a long lope. As he approached they pulled up, and, coming closer, Will saw the look of annoyance behind the welcome in Evarts' face. Sam's face was bland and ruddy and stolid, touched with a faint embarrassment, and Will came to a swift decision.

He pulled up beside John Evarts and folded his arms and leaned on the horn. "John," he murmured, "I'm an easy man to fire, but I like to hear it spoken."

John Evarts' mild face showed a faint distress, but he was too shrewd to pretend he didn't understand. He said quietly,

"You'll hear it spoken when I do, Will. We didn't want you along."

Will's glance shuttled to Sam, who regarded him steadily.

Evarts said, "You're no man to face Bide. That's all, Will."

To Sam, Will said, "You figured that out yourself, Sam?"

"I did," Sam said calmly.

Will shuttled his gaze to Evarts then. "Either I'm in this all the way or I'm out of it, John. Which will it be?"

"You're in it, Will."

"And either Sam runs D Cross or he runs Hatchet. Which?"

Evarts glanced uneasily at Sam, and Sam said calmly, "I'll run D Cross, Will."

"Then it's done," Will said mildly, straightening up.

Evarts wanted to say more, but the expression in Will's face suggested that the incident was closed. Evarts pulled his horse around, and they rode on down the faintly marked road.

A mile or so farther on they crossed a dim trail heading off to the north.

It was Will who noticed it first, and he reined up, peering at the ground. Evarts and

Sam reined up, too, and saw the wagon tracks. They came from east and turned north on the trail, and there were four riders beside the wagon.

Sam said presently, "You can't get a wagon through to Indian Ridge this way, can you?"

Will said, "No. You go ahead. I'll catch up."

"We'll all go," Evarts said abruptly, and he pulled his horse around.

Will was puzzled. This trail, he knew, led to a seep a mile or so through these hills. Beyond that was a rough, almost worthless country that lifted into the sorry range of Ray Cavanaugh's outfit below Indian Ridge.

He said nothing, however, as he fell in beside Evarts. They crossed a wooded rise, dropped down into a narrow tongue of alkali flats to the west, and then climbed a slope that held thick timber at its summit.

They topped the ridge, passing through its timber, and then reined in abruptly. Below them, and ahead, in a shallow bowl between ridges, there was a chuck wagon. The seep had kept the grass on the valley floor a deep green, and the chuck-wagon team and another pair of horses were loosely picketed on it.

Smoke spiraled up from the fire by the wagon, and three men were standing around it. The muffled sound of an ax regularly biting into wood came from among the trees of the opposite slope.

Will recognized the wagon immediately, and he glanced at Sam, who was looking at him.

Sam's startled glance shuttled to Evarts. "That's Bide's wagon off roundup."

Evarts' reply was unperturbed. "Save us a ride," he said and put his horse down the slope.

Will fell in behind Sam, who had let Evarts go ahead. One thing puzzled him; whoever was cutting wood up there was not cutting firewood. He was cutting green wood.

As they leveled off into the valley the three men beside the wagon parted, and Will saw that Bide, even as they approached, was talking quietly to the cook.

Evarts dismounted by the fire and said, "Morning, Bide," and Marriner nodded curtly. He was slighter than John Evarts, and had a kind of wiry toughness about him that had nothing to do with age. His black hair was streaked with gray at the temples, and he wore an old and torn Mackinaw minus its buttons. He was just off roundup, dusty and in need of a shave, but his dark eyes were bright, quick with an inborn insolence, and his glance first settled on Will, who was still mounted. This was the man who never had been afraid to fight Phil Evarts, and that first speculative glance at Will was a kind of tribute. It was Will's temper he was gauging and, finding it apparently placid, he looked at Evarts.

John squatted beside the fire, warming his hands, and asked, "Much of anything at Russian Springs, Bide?"

Bide said carefully, "Didn't look," and waited.

Will's glance traveled to the others. The cook stood with his back to the wagon, and against its wheel leaned a rifle within easy reach. The third man was a hand of Bide's. He noticed Sam studying Bide's man in his shrewd, inscrutable way. The chopping up the slope, Will noticed idly, had ceased.

"We were headed for there," Evarts said mildly.

"What for?" Bide didn't trouble to hide the contempt in his voice.

"I figured you might want that grass this

winter. Hatchet can't use it. Take it if you want it."

"I did," Bide said. Again he glanced at Will; again Will's expression was neutral.

Bide said with quiet scorn, "Hatchet's beginnin' to sing pretty small all of a sudden. How come?"

Evarts said reasonably, "No use hogging range you can't fill."

"Nor range you can." Bide stared scornfully at Evarts and spoke with open contempt now. "What else you givin' away, Evarts?"

"Nothing."

"So it's got to be taken from you," Bide jeered. "Well, we can do that too."

Evarts came full erect now, and again there was that look of helpless distress on his face. "What are you taking, Bide?"

"Take a look around you," Bide said quietly. "Cavanaugh's throwin' up a line shack here. His graze will join my piece there at the Springs. I'm helpin' him move in. I'll help others too."

The cook reached slowly for the rifle and picked it up. He was not looking at anyone.

Evarts, to his credit, did not look to either Sam or Will for help. He started around the fire, talking. "It won't join yours unless he fights for it," Evarts said flatly.

He came to a halt in front of Bide, who had not moved. Bide said with a slow insolence, "You got a job on your hands. Cavanaugh's cattle are already on Hatchet. The whole country's movin' in on you, Evarts. Didn't you know that?" John Evarts didn't answer.

"The whole gang of 'em—from under Indian Ridge, from the Salt Hills, and maybe from the Indigos. They're movin' in."

"You're lying," John Evarts said.

Bide smiled openly then. He turned his head and shouted up into the timber, "Ray! Come down here!"

There was a bright malice in his eyes as he looked beyond Evarts to Will, then, and returned his glance to Evarts.

The final piece of last night's puzzle slipped into place for Will now. Cavanaugh's laughter was understandable; he and Schultz had left town together, had met Bide in the night, and had moved over to the seep today from Russian Springs. He heard horses crashing down the brush of the slope, and gently, imperceptibly, he slipped his feet from the stirrup and pulled his mare back until Sam, still mounted, partially screened him from Marriner.

The cook and Cavanaugh's hand were watching Evarts, who was saying, "What outfits have moved in?" in an uncertain, halting voice. Bide didn't bother to answer.

Will glanced up the slope and saw Ray Cavanaugh and Russ Schultz, Marriner's foreman, break out of the timber. Cavanaugh had the carbine from his saddle scabbered across his pommel; Schultz had a rifle in his free hand.

When they hit the flats behind Bide the wagon screened them from Will's sight, and then he moved. He slipped noiselessly out of the saddle, vaulted the wagon tongue, and, yanking his gun from its holster, he pounded toward the rear of the wagon.

He heard Bide yell: "Watch him!" and then he rounded the end of the wagon, running full tilt and cutting in sharply.

He caught Cavanaugh just dismounted, just turning and swinging his carbine over the saddle, and he rammed into him with the point of his shoulder in a low, savage drive. It caught Cavanaugh in the side and drove him viciously into his horse. He heard

John Evarts' sharply excited voice saying, "Stand there, Schultz!" and then Cavanaugh brought down the butt of his carbine on Will's back. Will rolled away from him against the hind feet of Cavanaugh's horse, and Cavanaugh fell to his knees. Will saw his wry little face contorted with pain, trying to drag the rifle up to his shoulder.

The horse shied away from Will then, letting him fall on his back. Will saw the carbine lifting and he kicked wildly at it and hit it, and it went off. He had time now. He came to his knees just as Cavanaugh, rising, pumped a shell into his carbine. Will lunged and grabbed the barrel and turned full into Cavanaugh, hitting him with his back and yanking savagely on the gun. It wrenched free of Cavanaugh's hand, and Will threw it from him. He grabbed Cavanaugh by the shirt front now and drove three flat-handed blows into his face, the sound of their slapping as sharp as pistol shots. He flung him aside then with a savage sweep of his hand, and Cavanaugh hit the wheel of the wagon and fell under it, his head rapping sharply on the wheel spokes.

Breathing deeply, angrily, now, Will looked at the others. Evart's had his gun trained on Schultz, who stood just where he had dismounted, rifle slacking in his hand.

Sam had moved his horse in against the cook, pinning him so solidly against the wagon that he could not raise his rifle. Sam's gun was loosely trained on Bide's hand and on Bide himself.

Sam's careful glance was laid on Will now, and, seeing it, Will said with cold and wild malice, "Tell me again what satisfies Bide."

Sam wisely held his temper and said nothing. Cavanaugh crawled out from under the wagon. Will's hot, wild glance settled on John Evarts and shuttled from him to Bide, who stood bitterly watching this. Bide's face, however, was impassive; he was a gambler and he'd lost and now he was ready to pay up.

Will reached out and swung Cavanaugh around and shoved him toward Marriner. Cavanaugh tripped and fell, barely missing the fire, and Will did not notice him for watching Bide. "Take him back, Bide," Will drawled. "You can do better than him."

"There's always another time."

"But this is one you'll remember," Will said implacably. "You boys light out. Throw your guns down. Leave your horses."

Bide didn't even protest. For one still moment he regarded Will, reading the rage in him, and then he said bitterly, "You damned Injun. I'll remember it. Another time, Will."

Bide pulled his gun and threw it on the ground, then turned to the others and said, "Let's go." He looked at John Evarts now. "What about the wagon?"

"Leave it," Will said flatly.

"I'll remember that too," Bide said meagerly.

Without another word he started walking toward the near slope. Slowly, cursing, the others threw their guns on the grass and fell in behind him.

Will found his gun and holstered it then and glanced at Sam. "Much obliged," he said, his voice quieter now.

Sam and Evarts watched him as Will walked around to the tongue of the chuck wagon, lifted it, and shoved until the wheel was cramped.

Then Will got his rope, passed the loop around the hub of a rear wheel, and tossed the coil over the top of the wagon. Not until Will had picked up the free end of the rope and dallied it around the horn of his saddle did Sam's face lose its expression of disapproving curiosity. Then, as Will touched the mare with his spurs and the rope tightened and cut through the canvas, Sam understood. He looked swiftly to John Evarts, anger in his face. Evarts understood, too, and said nothing.

Will's mare leaned sturdily to the job. It took her two tries. On the second try, the wagon came up on the near wheels, balanced a moment, and then crashed over on top of the fire. Dismounting, Will saw that Bide and the others had paused halfway up the slope, watching this. He freed his rope and coiled it, and only after the wagon had caught fire did Bide turn and go on.

Will tramped around the wagon now and saw John Evarts regarding him grimly. "You can still fire me," he said truculently. "Go ahead," Evarts said.

Sam said calmly, "That's a mistake."

"Who made the first one?" Will said quickly, challengingly. Sam's temper didn't alter, and when Will was sure of it he walked over to his mare. He was about to mount when Sam's insistent voice came to him again. "Bide won't forget that, Will. I'm his neighbor. I know."

Will's eyes were suddenly brash now as he looked across the saddle at Sam. "Why, damn you, Sam, he isn't supposed to. I don't want him to."

Sam's squat face flushed a deep red now, and he and Will regarded each other for long seconds in utter silence. It was Will's farewell to caution, a warning both to Sam and John Evarts that he didn't want them to misunderstand.

Sam turned this over in his mind before he accepted it, afterward looking at Evarts. He said, "John, I'd fire him."

"He stays," Evarts said grimly. "I've had enough."

Chapter 3

The weather had broken, settling into a drizzle so cold that Sam Danfelser, paused in the doorway of the bank in Boundary, wished he had another coat to wear under his slicker for the ride out to D Cross. The water already pooled the fresh ruts, and about him was the small din of gutters emptying onto the wood awnings overhead and cascading into the street. There was the smell of wood smoke in the air and the town was alive again after calf branding; Sam should have felt exhilarated, and yet he felt oddly gloomy.

He stepped out into the slow afternoon rain and headed downstreet, wondering why his conference with old Kamerer at the bank had been so disappointing. In other years this simple ceremony—the cigar, the talk of prospects, the writing of the check in payment for his note—had been pleasant and solid. But this year it was different. Old Kamerer was worried. He had asked questions about Hatchet and tried, without making it too obvious, to find how Sam stood on the question of Hatchet. If Sam read the signs correctly the bank had decided, with that subtle instinct of self-preservation peculiar to banks, that Hatchet was done for. That whole belt of land from the Salt Hills to the Indigos would be broken up among new outfits who would require loans to stock it, and Kamerer was scheming.

Sam paused to look at the old Spanish saddle in the window of Doreen's saddle shop. He had examined it a dozen times and it held no further interest for him, but he stopped anyway, his thinking uninterrupted.

He should, he knew, be mightily concerned about the breakup of Hatchet, for John Evarts was aging, and when he died Celia would inherit it. If there was anything to inherit, that is.

And there wouldn't be. Up to yesterday John Evarts had played the poor hand dealt him with caution and wisdom, in spite of Will Ballard. But yesterday at the seep he had gone off the track, and that act would cost him Hatchet. Sam supposed darkly that there was a buried wild streak in all the Evarts, but that was all right. What wasn't right was that it took Will Ballard to bring it out, as he had brought it out in Phil, in Celia, and now in John. When Sam thought of Will he felt an angry bafflement that he couldn't name.

Sam turned away from the window and walked out to the edge of the plank walk, troubled and restless.

The Belle Fourche on the corner reminded him of a warming drink. He ducked under the tie rail and slogged across the muddy street, his burly torso almost splitting the slicker at each movement. Inside the saloon he stamped the mud from his boots, yanked off his Stetson, and swung it sharply to rid it of raindrops.

Only afterward did he look up, heading for the bar, to see Bide Marriner standing against it. Russ Schultz was with him, but they were not talking.

Sam saw Bide watching him in the backbar mirror, his dark face sardonic and watchful. Sam came up beside him and said, "A hell of a day to have to ride anywhere."

Bide said, "Especially after horses," and

looked directly at him. Bide hadn't shaved yet; he looked sleepy and irritable and keyed up, and Sam knew that Bide wasn't sure about the part he had played at the seep yesterday.

Sam said, "Whisky," to the bartender, and then half turned to Bide. "That wasn't my idea, Bide."

"You crowded George against the wagon, or he'd have stopped Will right there. You put a gun on me."

Sam nodded, his ruddy face holding a faint truculence. "I'll stop gunplay any time I get a chance. With you or anybody else, Bide."

Bide considered this a moment, watching Sam with hot, dark eyes. But Sam had lived on terms of moderate friendliness next to Bide in the Salt Hills for some years, and they had never quarreled. He counted on that, although Schultz's heavy, sullen face was unforgiving.

"All right," Bide said presently. "I think you would. Forget it. I'll buy you a drink."

"Bring it over to a table," Sam said. He shucked out of his slicker and tramped over to one of the tables near the front of the saloon. Bide spoke to Schultz and then followed Sam over to the table. After the bartender brought bottles and glasses Sam sat down and pulled out a worn brier whose bit was almost chewed through and packed it with tobacco from a buckskin sack he took from his hip pocket.

Seating himself, Marriner watched his deliberate movement with impatient, sardonic eyes, and finally blurted out, "I'm through with talk, Sam. I warn you." He toed over a chair and put his feet on the seat and regarded Sam suspiciously.

"You're not through yet," Sam contradicted him calmly. "Not if I can stop what might happen."

"You can't."

Sam didn't look at him. He lighted a match, puffed his pipe alight, and then carefully shook out the match. Then he regarded Marriner.

"I've never denied your rights, Bide. All I'd like to know is how much you want."

"So you can tell Phil's girl?" Bide asked quickly.

"She thinks you want all of it. I don't."

Bide was quiet, almost brooding, as he fingered his whisky glass. He sighed then and looked at Sam. "I don't know myself. I never thought of it." His feet came off the chair and he hunched forward, a fierce vehemence in his eyes, his voice. "I used to want to run cattle. But for five years all I been thinking about is getting even with Phil Evarts and Will Ballard. That's all I want."

Sam nodded slowly. "I can understand that."

Bide leaned back and said in the wry, bitter tones of anger, "Nobody can do that to me. Nobody."

"Suppose Will was counted out of it," Sam suggested.

Bide looked quickly at him, scowling. "Count him out. Go ahead and try it," he jeered.

"But suppose he was," Sam insisted. "I'm not saying he will be. I don't even know how he could be. But just suppose he was."

Bide thought a moment and then murmured, "Maybe that would be different."

"You've talked every ten-cow outfit under Indian Ridge into moving onto Hatchet grass. You think you could pull them back?"

Bide said sharply, "Are you talking a deal?"

Sam shook his head slowly, patiently. "I'm just talking. There's a way out of this.

There doesn't have to be any trouble." He paused. "Could you pull them back?"

Bide said slowly, "Not all the way. They don't want much, though."

Sam had his answer. It was oblique and not a promise, but to a man who understood Bide Marriner it was a great deal. And Sam was not a man to overplay his hand. He merely said, "It might be a good thing, Bide. You see," he added quietly, "someday I'll marry Celia Evarts. I wouldn't want to have to take on all of Indian Ridge and you too."

Bide watched him thoughtfully as he filled their glasses and shoved Bide's toward him. Bide took his and said mildly, "I'll talk about that when Will Ballard's licked."

"Sure, sure," Sam said. He lifted his glass and they drank, and afterward Sam stood up and put on his slicker. Bide drifted back to the bar and Sam went out.

It was still raining, but as Sam walked down to the livery stable and saddled his horse he felt strangely relieved. He was right about knowing Bide; a man could live at peace with him if he only understood the conditions.

Sam rode down the main street, reins

looped over his saddle horn, and he buttoned his slicker collar. He looked at the western sky and saw a break in the gray over the Indigos and thought maybe it would clear off tonight.

At the edge of town he passed a pair of kids on a plooding old roan mare, the lard buckets in which they carried lunch to school suspended from the saddle horn and banging at each slogging step the old mare took.

Ahead of him Bill Donovan's two kids from out on Alkali Flat rode out of the schoolyard headed for home.

Sam looked idly at the frame schoolhouse where the usually hard-packed yard, now a soupy mud, was scarred with the tracks of the children and their horses. And then the thought came to him so abruptly that he reined up in the middle of the street.

Presently he kneed his horse over to the schoolyard and sought the shed out by the fence. Dismounting in its shelter beside another horse, he started back for the schoolhouse, paused, and went back to gather up an armload of cut wood stacked in the shed.

He tramped into the schoolroom, and

Lottie Priest, who was sweeping out, looked up as he entered.

Sam dumped the wood by the stove and said, "That's my early training."

Lottie laughed. "You must have had a better teacher than I am, Sam. How are you?"

She came over to him, and Sam took off his hat and they shook hands. He had known Lottie for years and liked her, although he seldom saw her except at dances.

Lottie sat on one of the desk benches, but Sam, whose thick bulk made this schoolroom seem almost miniature, settled himself gingerly on top of a desk opposite her.

"I dropped your mare off at home," Sam said. "Will said to thank you."

"How was calf branding?"

Sam said matter-of-factly, watching her, "Not like old times, when Hatchet ruled the roost."

Lottie said quickly, "Sam, I heard this morning there'd been trouble between Bide and Will yesterday."

She's worried, Sam thought, and he nodded. "There's always trouble when Will and Bide meet. This time Will set him afoot."

Lottie didn't comment, but her face showed distress, and this fact encouraged Sam. Because he was a direct man, Sam came straight to the point now. "I was wondering, Lottie. Has Will ever thought of leaving Hatchet?"

"He wouldn't consider it, Sam."

Sam said shrewdly, "But you'd like him to?"

Lottie hesitated and then nodded slowly.

"Let me give you some advice," Sam said. He smiled, to make it seem friendly, which it was. "You didn't ask for it, but I'm giving it to you, anyway. It's time you got him out of there, Lottie."

Alarm flooded into Lottie's eyes. "What is it, Sam? Has anything happened?"

"Nothing much, maybe. I'll let you judge. This morning Will and John each took a couple of Hatchet hands and split up. Do you know where they rode? To kick off every outfit that's moved onto Hatchet grass."

"What outfits? When was this?" Lottie asked quickly.

"I forgot to tell you," Sam murmured. "Bide's got most of the country except me to move in on Hatchet. Will is starting with that bunch from under Indian Ridge. When he's kicked them off he'll move to bigger game. He'll get to Bide." Lottie half rose and then sank down behind the desk again. With sudden perception Sam sensed that Lottie had betrayed in that one movement her inability to sway Will. He said, "That's a large order, even if he wades through the lot of them to Bide." He added calmly, "Bide's got Russian Springs now."

Lottie didn't answer, and Sam shifted his weight a little. His oily slicker peeled away from the desk top, diverting him for an instant.

Then he said, "Lottie, you're not the kind to dodge things. I think you know this anyway." He paused, isolating this. "There'd be no trouble here if Will would move. Bide would tame."

"Will says he wouldn't."

Sam shook his head. "Bide lived to get even with Phil Evarts, and now Will has taken Phil's place. When he hasn't got Will to fight, he's like any other man."

Lottie stroked the smooth desk with her hand, and she was not looking at Sam. He knew he had said enough, only he could not resist a last telling point.

He came off the desk and said, "You're the schoolteacher, Lottie. You remember that one about it's better to be a live coward than a dead hero."

"It's just the other way around in the schoolbooks, Sam."

"No," Sam said gently. "You don't believe it's the other way around either, do you?"

Lottie held his glance for a few seconds and then said quietly, "No, Sam. I want him alive."

"Then you'd better be quick about it," Sam said gently. He nodded to her and went out.

Chapter 4

This camp puzzled Will. He and Ike Adams were bellied down in the mud of a ridge top, a piñon screening them from the camp in the draw below. The rain fell steadily, persistently, and the two men in cracked slickers down there in the scrub cedar were trying, and not very successfully, to rustle wood for their fire. A tarp strung between two of the cedars shelterd their outfit, and their underfed horses—two saddle animals and a pack horse—were foraging dismally and halfheartedly down the draw.

Ike said, "Hell, they ain't even bothered to put out a guard," and he looked at Will, puzzled. They had seen a scattering of gaunted strange cattle at the mouth of this draw that opened out from the Indian Ridge country and had made a careful circle to pull in above the camp. Will had expected to see more men, and careful men, for stealing range had never been anything but a serious matter. These men seemed concerned about nothing except how to keep warm. It was a curious procedure for an outfit at open war with Hatchet. For it was war now, after what Bide had said yesterday.

Will said, "We'll walk down and brace 'em."

"I dunno," Ike said cautiously. He had ridden with Hatchet when it really knew trouble and had learned caution the hard way. He was a middle-aged man, taciturn to surliness, except where work was concerned. He had a fierce unthinking loyalty for Hatchet which, for him, meant Will. He shook his head. "This don't look right."

He pushed himself to his knees and said, "I'll drop down-canyon a ways and walk up to their horses. You drift down behind 'em."

Will nodded, and Ike set off, his boots balling up with the greasy mud before he had taken ten steps.

Will waited, watching the pair by the fire. He could place neither them nor the Star 22 brand on their horses, which was not the brand the strange cattle had carried. But he was certain of what he would do with them, and John Evarts had agreed.

He shuttled his glance down the canyon where the horses were grazing. Now he saw Ike come down off the slope and, once in the open, walk up slowly to the pack horse that stood watching him alertly.

Two men at the fire had seen Ike now, and one of them yelled, "Hey!"

Ike paid no attention, walking up to the horse as if he had not heard. The two men looked at each other, and then the nearest man dropped the dead branch he had just picked up and started toward Ike. The second, squatted by the fire, rose and hurried to join him.

They walked below Will, and when they were past he rose, rifle in hand, and started silently down the slippery slope. He hit the canyon floor behind them, and then they halted in front of Ike.

Will heard one of them say, "What're you lookin' for?"

Ike had reached the pack horse now, and he scratched its nose, and Will heard him answer, "What you got under those slickers, boys?"

Will came on, walking quietly, and again Ike spoke. "Just leave 'em buttoned and take a look behind you."

One of the men turned and saw Will, who was holding his cocked rifle hip-high. The other one turned a moment later, and they watched Will approach.

Will saw they were brothers; they had the same long faces and bleach eyes, and in both their faces was an instant, sober alertness. They were a young and hungry-looking pair, but they eyed him levelly, with more respect than fear.

Will murmured dryly, "Go ahead. Tell me you don't know where you are."

The older one shook his head slowly. "I know too damn well where we are, mister."

The honest reply puzzled Will momentarily, and he did not speak.

The younger one, with a kind of wry humor, said to his brother without looking at him, "He the one they said would be so busy he couldn't get to all of us?"

The older one smiled embarrassedly but did not answer. He watched Will carefully, alertly.

Will said, "Where was this?"

The older one tilted his head toward the mountains. "Back in Ten Mile."

"Who said it?"

"Redheaded fellow in the saloon there."

Will seemed to ponder this while Ike watched him with a deepening alarm. Will said then, "You're not from around here."

The older brother shook his head. "We come up with one of them Indian trail herds. They paid off on the reservation, and we took our wages in cull stuff. Figured to drive across the mountains and find us some grass, and back there in Ten Mile we heard about this outfit."

Ike spoke with a surly truculence. "Heard what?"

The older one looked at his brother and shrugged. "This outfit was s'posed to be bustin' up. They said there was all the grass a man wanted, just for the takin'."

Ike said grimly, "There is, if you can take it." He came up to the younger one, ripped open his slicker, and lifted out a gun. The second man held his arms away and let Ike do the same to him. They both kept watching Will, however, for a clue to what would happen to them.

Will's face was impassive, but a slow anger smoldered in his eyes. It did not touch these men, for in their places he would have done the same. His anger was at Bide and his sly, tireless schemings. Ten Mile was up in the Indigos at the end of a logging road. There was a rickety hotel there, the old logging-camp bunkhouse, along with a saloon and a store. It was Red Courteen's town, out of which he and his men peddled whisky to the Indians and smuggled the beef they received in payment out of the country. A furtive trade in stolen horses and cattle was carried on there, and a few small outfits under Indian Ridge who were more than a day's ride from Boundary traded there. Red Courteen had always been too wise to provoke Hatchet, but now that was changed too. Bide had persuaded him, and Red, in turn, had sent on these two ragged punchers who only wanted grass to give them a start. They had risked the gamble and lost.

Will let his rifle swing to his side. "Let 'em go, Ike."

The outrage in Ike's face was immediate, and he only stared at Will.

Will asked curtly, "What's your name?"

The older one said, "Mel Young. Brother's name's Jim." Only now that Will had let them go did he seem ashamed and somehow eager to please.

Will wiped a muddy hand on his slicker, framing his orders to them, and he was aware that Ike was watching with fierce disapproval. He looked at the younger brother, who grinned faintly, his sole gesture of thanks for letting them go.

A sudden thought struck Will. "Those your cattle down-canyon?"

Jim Young nodded. Will wheeled and looked back at their outfit, which was small enough that a pack horse could carry it. When he faced them again his mind was made up. "What do you do now?"

"Get off your range," Mel said soberly.

"Want grass for your stuff?"

The two brothers looked at each other, and Jim Young said cautiously, "Sure."

"Want it bad enough to work for nothing? I'll feed you and put you up, but there's no pay in it. You can run your stuff along with ours."

Mel said immediately, "Hell, yes, we'll take it."

"We're having trouble, you understand."

"We'll take that too," Jim Young said.

While Ike held his surly silence Will gave them directions to Hatchet. After their guns had been returned he and Ike left them and climbed the slope in the still-falling rain and sought their horses. Ike paused as he was about to mount and looked at Will. "Know what a rawhider is, Will?"

Will shook his head in negation.

"They travel in wagons, whole famblies of 'em," Ike said wryly. "They'll clean a country quicker'n locusts. Steal you blind and deef. All their sorry gear they patch with rawhide."

Will frowned, and Ike spat and said mildly, "Notice that youngest kid's gun handle was tied with rawhide?"

"No."

Ike said gloomily, "You're goin' to be sorry you didn't run 'em out of the country. I'd sooner trust Red Courteen than them two."

Will said mildly, patiently, "We need a crew if we're going to fight, Ike. That's one way to get one."

When John Evarts saw the first scattering of cattle in the dripping timber, he grunted with satisfaction. Bide had been right yesterday when he said Ray had moved his stuff down onto Hatchet grass.

A Hatchet hand who had ridden over for a confirming look pulled up beside Evarts and the other Hatchet hand. "They're Cavanaugh's, all right."

"Gather 'em up," Evarts ordered.

For two hours he combed the surrounding country with his men in the steady rain, and when they met they had seventy head of cattle bunched on the wet flats.

Evarts said, "Take them back to the corrals, and we'll wait for Cavanaugh to show up."

He and Will had agreed last night that it was impossible for Hatchet, undermanned and weak, to push every outfit off Hatchet grass. An easier way, and just as effective, would be to gather up all strange cattle, hold them at the ranch pasture, and face the men who came to redeem them.

Of one of the men now he asked, "Who has that place over there in the hills closest—Kennedy?"

"Back yonder," the puncher said, nodding toward Indian Ridge.

"He's all right, isn't he?"

"Wes?" The puncher grinned. "He's too tired to steal, I reckon."

"You boys get along," Evarts said. "I'll catch up with you."

He turned his pony north toward the hills as his men got the bedraggled cattle moving toward home.

A change had come over John Evarts since yesterday, and he scarcely knew what to make of it himself. He knew one thing however: for the first time since coming to Hatchet he had broken through Will Ballard's reserve. He knew what had done it, too, knew the second it took place. It was when he had given his unspoken consent yesterday for Will to go ahead with the disarming of Bide and his men and the wrecking of the chuck wagon. Up to that moment he had been headed in one direction; at that moment, he swerved, and immediately Will Ballard was with him. It was that simple really.

He shifted in the wet saddle and wondered why he did not find it uncomfortable. Presently he dropped down into the valley where the argument had taken place yesterday.

He reined up and looked at it curiously. There was the chuck wagon on its side, its canvas vanished, its bed gutted, but its frame and two wheels holding together to mark the time the rain started and doused the fire. Pots, pans, and canned goods littered the ground.

Evarts regarded it wonderingly, and his mild face, wet and flushed now in the cold rain, reflected a grim pleasure. He wanted to fix this lonely scene in his mind, because it was a milestone in his life. If Bide had been content with claiming Russian Springs instead of overplaying his hand by coming to Ray Cavanaugh's help, things would have gone their worrisome way. For John Evarts wasn't a coward and he knew he wasn't. It was just that up to yesterday he had believed, against Will's quiet contradiction, that Bide had a normal man's hunger for land and power whipped a little raw by Phil Evarts' victories. Now he knew Bide's appetite went beyond that. He wanted Hatchet brought to its knees, so he could take it, and John was going to fight him—now.

John had only a vague idea of where Kennedy's place was and, feeling his way into this rough country, he came across a trail that swung a little west through the scrub timber. He followed its lift for three hours until it let onto a long meadow, at the end of which he could see a shack and outbuildings.

As he approached Evarts looked around

the place and grimaced. A brush corral, a pole-and-brush shed, and a crude log shack made up the place, and it was a dozen outfits like this that Marriner had enlisted to help him in his fight against Hatchet.

Coming into the yard, Evarts saw a man step out onto the porch and lean against the post, watching him.

Evarts reined up and said, "How are you, Kennedy?"

"Pretty good, Mr. Evarts," Kennedy drawled. He had the reputation of being a garrulous young man with a kind of shiftless, cheerful foolishness about him. His vest and shirt were close to tatters, his boots cracked and barely holding together. But in spite of his smile, his air of foolish unconcern, there was an uneasiness about him that Evarts couldn't fathom. This impression was strengthened by the fact that Kennedy didn't ask him to step down, although it was the custom of the country and the day was foul.

Kennedy just watched him uneasily, hands in pockets.

Evarts said, "You're a neighbor to Cavanaugh, aren't you?"

Kennedy nodded cautiously.

"Ever see him?"

"Now and then, Mr. Evarts. Just every once in a while, you might say."

"Next time you see him give him a message for me, will you?"

Kennedy looked vastly relieved. He grinned uneasily and said, "Sure."

"Tell him we're holding his cattle at the house. If he wants them he can come and get them."

Kennedy said quickly. "I'll tell him. Sure thing, Mr. Evarts."

Evarts nodded and was about to pull his horse around when a man stepped out of the shack behind Kennedy. Kennedy wheeled, as if to stop him, and was shoved roughly aside.

Ray Cavanaugh stood there, a rifle held at his side. In the first brief glimpse of him Evarts thought he was drunk. His tight, tough face was flushed, his hair awry, and he was in his sock feet. Then he coughed. He did not cease watching Evarts with his wild, bloodshot eyes, but his coughing, deep and pulpy, almost doubled him over. He dragged in a couple of deep, almost choking breaths of air, and when he spoke his voice was rough and hoarse.

"Get down off that horse!"

Evarts just watched him in silence. "You're sick."

"Damn right I am," Cavanaugh said. "I footed it for five hours in that rain to make it here. You're goin' to do the same." Evarts had a swift, momentary pity for the man, and then it vanished. A man accepted the consequences of his own acts, and Cavanaugh must accept his. There was a new stubbornness in John Evarts as he shook his head.

"I don't think so."

Cavanaugh raised his rifle almost to his shoulder. "Have I got to shoot you off that horse?"

"Yes, you do."

For a moment the two men looked at each other, and then Evarts saw the maniac rage mount in Cavanaugh's eyes. A cold dismay struck him, and he yanked his horse around, seeing the gun lift to Cavanaugh's shoulder as he wheeled.

He never heard the shot. Something smashed his breath out of him. He tasted mud, and that was all.

As Evarts slipped to the ground Kennedy lunged for the rifle and wrenched it out of

Cavanaugh's hands. He dropped it, plunging off the porch into the slippery yard. He fell once, rose and raced on, and when he reached Evarts he knelt, pulled him off his back, and turned him over. A thin ribbon of blood licked out from the corner of Evarts' muddy mouth, spread fuzzily as the rain touched it, and vanished down behind his jaw.

Kennedy, in panic, shook him, and when Evarts' head rolled loosely he dropped him. Coming to his feet in the rain, the full horror of it held him motionless a moment, and then he turned and looked at Cavanaugh on the porch.

"You killed him."

Cavanaugh stepped down and came across to him, his bare feet leaving big splayed tracks in the mud. Both men stood there staring at Evarts, and then Cavanaugh whispered, "O Jesus." Kennedy didn't even hear him.

Cavanaugh wasn't mad any more. The memory of the bitter humiliation, of Will Ballard's contemptuous beating, of his wild rage at anything Hatchet was gone, and only fear remained. His sick mind raced ahead now, picturing the chain of frightening events this shooting would put in movement, and he shivered uncontrollably.

"You saw him," he said fiercely to Kennedy. "He was pullin' his gun on me! I had to do it!"

Kennedy looked at him and said without spirit, "He wasn't goin' for his gun."

"Listen," Cavanaugh pled hoarsely. "He was goin' for his gun. I saw him!"

Kennedy just looked at him, the horror still in his eyes.

Cavanaugh fought for a grip on himself. Like a small snake creeping experimentally from under a stone, an idea, furtive and guileful, was coming to life in his sick brain. The rain beat down through his sandy hair, cooling the fever in him.

"Listen, Wes," he said. His voice had lost its panic and now had an ugliness to it. 'You're in this too."

Kennedy raised both hands and took a step backward. "Oh no," he said quickly. "Not me. I never shot him. I never had a gun. I never even saw it."

"I'll tell Ballard you did."

Kennedy just stared at him. Then he turned and raced for the porch. Scooping up the rifle, he trained it on Cavanaugh and came slowly and uncertainly toward him in the steady rain. "You ain't dragging me into this, Ray. No sir."

Cavanaugh said tauntingly, "Go ahead and shoot."

Kennedy licked his lips and regarded Cavanaugh with helpless horror in which there was no anger even.

"Lever a shell in. You forgot that," Cavanaugh taunted.

Kennedy's gun slacked off then, and he almost wailed. "What'll we do, Ray? What'll we do?"

Cavanaugh knew he had his man now. Wes Kennedy was a trifling man without the courage to protect himself. "Get out of the rain first," Cavanaugh said.

"But—"

"He's dead, ain't he?" Cavanaugh snarled.

He shouldered past Kennedy and went up to the porch and into the shack. He wrenched a dirty blanket from the bunk and threw it around him and came out onto the porch. Kennedy was standing there, his gaze intent and afraid and somehow begging.

Cavanaugh smothered his shivering and said, "How they goin' to know he's dead if they can't find him?"

Kennedy shook his head, didn't answer.

"We got to bury him up in the timber," Cavanaugh said. "This rain'll hide the hole. It'll hide his tracks comin' up here."

Kennedy licked his lips and said, "No, Ray. No. Not on my place. Ballard'll kill me if he finds out."

"How's he goin' to find out?" Cavanaugh snarled. He coughed then, gagging on the violence of it. Afterward, he steadied himself against the wall and said to Kennedy, with a confidence he did not feel himself, "Get a shovel."

Kennedy didn't move. Cavanaugh, afraid and desperate now, walked up to him and cuffed him across the face with the flat of his palm.

Then he reached out and grasped the lapels of Kennedy's vest and shook him violently. The blanket fell off Cavanaugh's shoulders.

"You damn jughead, we're in this together, don't you see that! You're goin' to bury him up there and I'm goin' to watch you. Then I'm goin' home. And you ain't goin' to light out from here; you can't! Will Ballard will hunt you to China!"

He paused and let go Kennedy's lapels,

and Kennedy just looked at him with naked fear.

"Bluff it out!" Cavanaugh snarled. "Nobody can prove anythin'. Now get a shovel!"

Chapter 5

Sam left D Cross early and dropped down through the timbered foothills toward Alkali Flats. The ground mist was so thick on the flats after the rain that it seemed a pearl-gray sea. Sam rode briskly, for he had ground to cover this morning.

Around nine o'clock Sam crossed Bandoleer Creek and was presently off his own grass and onto Hatchet range, which adjoined it to the west. This was a waterless stretch, dry in the summer months, and it marked the boundary beyond which his cattle could not graze. This dry range stretched from Indian Ridge south and marked the west boundary of Bide's range, his own, Ladder, next to him, and Six X, next to Ladder. The only water on it was Russian Springs, which Bide had seized, and a few dug wells farther south, which would not water a dozen head of cattle. Bide had seized the single bridge through which he could move deeper into Hatchet. The dug wells he had not bothered with, and it was the range around these wells that Sam was curious about this morning.

The sun had broken through now to drive off the ground mist, but it was not warm yet, and the wet smell of cold spring earth remained. As Sam approached the range around the dug well he saw his first cattle and rode over to get a closer look. He saw the Ladder branded on their steaming coats. It was as he expected. Allan, at Ladder, had no especial quarrel with Hatchet, but he was, nevertheless, not going to let Bide Marriner gobble all of Hatchet graze. If Bide moved farther Allan would move too. Sam had a moment of sullen anger then as he thought of his position in this business. He could not gracefully take any Hatchet range, but if it turned out that Hatchet couldn't push the others off he stood to lose a lot of free grass by his hesitancy. His hands were tied.

Cutting north now, Sam made for Russian Springs, but before he reached it he had an answer to his question. Bide's cattle had moved in all right. Moreover, Bide had line riders out, for Sam had had to pull back into timber to escape being seen by a rider leisurely skirting the hills.

Afterward Sam turned west toward Hatchet, a restlessness upon him now. Bide had moved, and Ladder, not to be outdone, had pushed in too. Farther south Six X had undoubtedly done the same, since Ladder had set the example. Those, with his own brand, accounted for the outfits in the Salt Hills flanking Hatchet. The rabble under Indian Ridge had undoubtedly moved in, and if they had, it argued that the small outfits in the Indigos, in spite of their truce with Hatchet, would push their boundaries down to include a chunk of Hatchet. Now was the time to act, Sam knew. And he had the proof for John and Celia that it was necessary, for Sam still thought he could sway John.

He rode into Hatchet after noon, and when he saw the cattle grazing in the horse pasture he grimaced. They were Cavanaugh's, mixed with a few from other outfits, he noticed, and he rode up to the house and dismounted. In spite of his hurry this morning, Sam had taken time out to shave, and his face, flushed with the ride, was even more high-colored than usual. He tramped down the veranda, stopped at the kitchen window and peered in, and then stepped inside.

The smell of baking struck him like a soft, delicious pillow as he stepped in. Celia, kneeling by the oven door, looked up and smiled and said, "Isn't that just like me? I bake the day all the wood's wet."

Sam threw his hat in a chair and came over to the table where cookies were laid out on an old newspaper. He picked one up and took a bite out of it, watching Celia.

Her cheeks were flushed with the heat from the stove, and her black hair was awry. She shoved the cookies in the oven and stood up and took a deep breath.

"These are good," Sam said.

"They're awful, and you know it," Celia said, almost tartly. She looked at Sam now.

Sam said, "What's eating you?"

"John's gone," Celia said calmly. "I had to do something to keep from thinking about it."

Sam's hand, clutching a second cookie, was arrested in mid-air. He said blankly, "Gone?"

"He didn't come home last night," Celia

said. She sank into a chair and brushed a wisp of black hair from her cheek and regarded Sam levelly. "He left the men yesterday afternoon. Said he was going to Kennedy's. He isn't home yet, and Will's ridden over there this morning."

"Why Kennedy's?"

"I don't know," Celia said wearily. She leaned back in her chair and stared at the opposite window, her gray eyes troubled. Sam put the cookie in his mouth, and when he had swallowed it he said easily, "He was probably wet and cold enough to stay the night."

"Do you think so?" Celia asked dryly.

Sam frowned. Celia was sharp this morning, and that meant she was worried. He debated whether to bring up his business, now that John wasn't here, and decided abruptly that he would. Now that Celia and John agreed, maybe John would listen to her. And right now she could transfer some of her absurd concern over John to something that really needed it.

He came over and put a foot on the chair beside her and folded his arms on his knees.

"Celia, what are those cattle doing in the horse pasture?"

"They're the one's we've seized on Hatchet grass."

Sam grunted. "You can't keep 'em. Will knows that."

"He doesn't want to. But he can make it mighty uncomfortable for the men who come to claim them."

Sam smiled grimly. "He's got a job ahead of him if he goes through with it." When Celia didn't say anything he said heavily, "Or didn't you know your whole east range is being taken over by Bide and Ladder and Six X?" He didn't have proof that Case at Six X had moved in, but he was sure he had.

"We expected that."

"I know. What are you going to do about it?"

"You heard Will say the other night. When we get these little outfits off our backs we're going to work on the others."

"When?"

Celia shrugged.

"Ladder cattle are around the wells now."

Celia said with exasperation, "Sam, you can't be subtle. What are you trying to say?"

Sam said stubbornly, "I'm trying to stop this before it gets started. Allan will wait until Bide's moved in farther than he has, and then he'll move farther. What about the outfits in the Indigos too? Harve Garretson and the others?"

"They've always been friends with Hatchet," Celia said hotly. "They won't take a foot of Hatchet range!"

"So Will thinks," Sam said heavily. "My hunch is that the Salt Hills and Indigos outfits will be standing in your garden patch arguing who gets it unless you do something."

"What more can we do?" Celia asked resentfully.

Sam should have seen the warning light in Celia's rain-gray eyes, but he was not a sharp man in the ways of women. He had a point to make, and he went at it in the only way he knew, which was head on.

"I saw Bide in town yesterday. Talked with him."

Celia kept ominously quiet.

"There's just one thing keeping Bide in this fight."

"Hatchet's range, of course."

"No." Sam paused. "It's Will."

Celia said with a deceptively mild curiosity, "How did he happen to say that?"

"I asked him what would satisfy him," Sam explained. "He said he hadn't even thought of it. All he wanted was to get Will out of the way."

Celia came slowly to her feet now, and when she spoke her voice held only the faintest undercurrent of anger. "In other words, you arranged a deal with Bide. He'd quit if Will would go?"

Sam straightened up, nodding. "Yes, you might call it that. That was understood, kind of. It——"

"On whose authority did you do this?" Celia asked. The anger was really out now, and Sam looked startled.

"Why—nobody's," he said resentfully. "I tried to get a basis for settling this row, is all."

"And the basis is that Will goes?" Celia's tone was one of contempt and scorn.

Sam looked at her narrowly, not angry, but trying to reach back of her anger.

"Who's Will that Hatchet needs him so bad you and John will wreck it to keep him?" he asked slowly.

"Only Dad's friend! My friend and John's! The best cattleman this country ever saw!" Celia flared.

Sam's square face altered slightly. "I'd always thought," he said dryly, "the sun could come up without his help. Maybe I was wrong."

"That's not fair, Sam!"

"I always thought he could be wrong sometimes," Sam went on with dogged sarcasm. "Maybe I was wrong again."

"But you're wrong now, and Will's right," Celia said instantly.

"Oh." Sam just stared at her, as if he'd seen something new in her. "I knew you were the one that kept Will on here. I thought, though, if it ever came to a choice between Will and Hatchet, Will would go."

Celia said hotly. "If *I* have anything to do with it Will won't go! So forget it, Sam!"

Sam just looked at her curiously. "Sure. Sure," he said softly, mildly. "But not before John knows this."

"I'll tell him," Celia said defiantly.

Sam regarded her curiously. She was stirred, really angry, over what he'd said about Will. Talk of Will had always been avoided between them, usually because Sam didn't like him and Celia did. He had excused this in her on the grounds of sentiment. Will had helped bring Hatchet to power, and old Phil, who was like Will, treated him as a son. But there was a limit to sentiment, and this was it. Sam knew an honest bafflement now. Will was only a foreman—smart, but too reckless and unstable—and he stood in the way of Hatchet. Yet Celia, who would own Hatchet and who would be his wife, couldn't see this.

A sudden unwanted suspicion came to Sam then, and he put it scornfully aside as beneath consideration. Celia was watching him with a defiance in her eyes that Sam did not care to bait. He picked up his hat and said quietly, "I'll be getting on."

Celia's anger melted then. She came over to him and put her hands on his shoulders and buried her face in his chest and was quiet a moment.

She said presently, "I'm sorry, Sam. I— guess I'm worried about Uncle John."

Sam said soberly, "You've got a tongue."

Celia looked at him and smiled fleetingly. "I guess you'll have to take that along with the rest of me, Sam." She turned away from him and saw the cookies on the table.

"Want to take some home?" she asked.

"I guess not," Sam said stolidly. "They're not very good." When Celia turned to look at him he was putting on his hat, oblivious to her gaze. "I'll be getting on. So long," he said placidly.

"So long, Sam."

When he was gone she kept staring at the door. She heard him ride out, and only then did she move.

She came up to the table, picked up a cookie, and nibbled judiciously on it. Then she gathered up the paper by its corners, went to the stove, lifted the lid, and threw the cookies in the fire. Those in the oven followed.

Will and Jim Young rode into Kennedy's place around noon. Kennedy was spading the muddy vegetable patch in front of his shack.

As they approached Will saw that Kennedy was almost bogged down in mud. His boots were balled with it; his hands and forearms were caked, and the yard between the patch and the porch looked as if a herd of horses had been driven across it.

Jim Young drawled quietly, "He likes draggin' mud, looks like."

Will nodded agreement. Kennedy appeared not to see them until they were almost into the yard. Then he straightened up, leaned on his spade, and watched them approach.

Will reined up just outside the patch and looked at the furrows of mud and said, "What's your hurry, Wes?"

Kennedy spat and tramped across to them and jammed his spade in the mud. "I tell you, Will. I got so sick of the inside of that shack while it was rainin' that I just made up some outside work this mornin'."

He grinned and looked at Will, and then his glance slid away. He rubbed his face with his palm and got dirt in his mouth and spat it out, and then glanced nervously at Jim Young. The Texan was watching him with a veiled curiosity. Wes said cordially, "Howdy."

"Howdy," Jim said.

Will looked around the place and then returned his gaze to Kennedy. "You were here yesterday, Wes?"

"That's right. Lost some cattle?"

"Why, no," Will murmured. He was looking at Wes, and his green eyes were watchful, probing. Kennedy, seeing it, was afraid of this big man; he was so afraid of him that he had declined to join Marriner in moving onto Hatchet. And now, with this unbearable secret locked inside, he had to face him. Cavanaugh had told him to bluff it out, but Kennedy had known even then that this was impossible. And now Will had come, and his horse was standing almost on the spot where John Evarts had fallen and which Kennedy had tried to cover up.

He waited, and when Will just kept watching him his glance raised to Will and fell instantly. He studied the handle of the spade and he felt sweat begin to bead his face.

"Anything wrong, Wes?" Will asked mildly. Kennedy made himself look at Will.

"Wrong?" He cleared his throat, pulling his voice down from an uncertain treble to its normal register. "Nothin' wrong with me, Will. Why?"

"You look kind of worried."

"Why should I?" Kennedy forced his voice into feigning anger. He looked sternly at Will and again he couldn't hold Will's glance. He looked instead at Jim Young and blurted, "Who's this fella, Will?"

Will said mildly, implacably, "John Evarts headed this way yesterday, Wes. Seen him?"

Kennedy closed his eyes, afraid he would faint, and then he dragged his glance up to Will again. "I ain't seen him, Will. Why would he come here?"

Will said gently, ignoring the question, "You're sure, Wes?"

"I been here all the time!" Wes cried.

Will reached down with one swift movement and gathered in Kennedy's shirt and hauled him roughly against his leg. "You're kind of worried, Wes," he drawled.

"I'll tell you! I'll tell you!" Kennedy bawled.

When Will let go Kennedy's knees gave way and he fell. Dragging himself to his feet, his mind was working with a panicked swiftness. He knew without thinking that if he told Will the truth he was a dead man.

He reached out and steadied himelf against Will's bay horse and said, "Will, I stole a Hatchet cow," and he looked at Will.

The blazing disappointment in Will's eyes was like a flag of hope to Kennedy, and his words began to tumble out uncontrollably.

"I done it, Will; figured you wouldn't miss one more after all you lost last winter, so I stole her. I butchered her and buried the hide and I got the meat. But I'll pay you back. I swear I will. I got a cow you can have. She's right close to Hatchet now, and I'll drive her over to your place. I——"

"Quit it," Will said in weary disgust.

Kennedy stopped talking. He was almost afraid to breathe as he tried to read the expression on Will's face. It was one of bitter disappointment and puzzlement.

"Evarts wasn't here?" Will asked.

"No, sir," Kennedy said flatly. He knew that Will had accepted the explanation of his fear, and he had the cunning now to see that talk would save him, not silence.

"Will, you ain't goin' to hold this against me, are you, if I give you a cow? I swear I got one you can have, and I'll do anythin' you say to make up for it. I'll even let you have——"

"All right," Will said impatiently. He looked at Jim Young and shook his head once and turned his horse around.

Kennedy stood there, breathing softly, looking at the ground, knowing Will was watching him, hoping against hope that he would not have to look at Will again.

Will said wearily, "Bring a cow over, Wes."

"Yes sir," Wes said, still not looking up.

He heard the two horses start to move and then he raised his glance. He watched Will and the Hatchet hand ride off out of sight. Then he started to shiver and he could not stop.

I got to get out of here, he thought wildly. *He'll be back.*

He started to run and then hauled up and looked in the direction Will had gone, as if Will might be watching.

He sauntered, almost, toward the brush shed where his pony was corralled.

And no power in the world could have made him lift his eyes to the timbered slope above where John Evarts lay in the fresh grave.

Once in the shed, he went about saddling his pony with a wild and panicked haste.

In the timber Will said, "What do you think?" to Jim Young.

The Texan shook his head. "He's too triflin' to hurt a man."

It was what Will thought, too, only he wasn't sure. In the beginning he'd been so dead certain that Kennedy was hiding knowledge of John Evarts that he would have staked his life on it—and then the confession of cow stealing changed that. And yet he wasn't quite satisfied.

He said impatiently, "We'll take a look, Jim." He gave Jim instructions to cut for sign on the trails to west. He himself was taking the other side of this trail to Kennedy's.

He dropped down the timbered slope a mile and turned off a dim trail that worked deeper in toward Indian Ridge and Cavanaugh's to the east.

As he rode along it the feeling came upon him that this was useless. The long hours of rain had washed this country clean of sign, and John Evarts had disappeared in the middle of that rain. The trail here held the ridges of old tracks, but they might be a month or a day old.

Presently he came to a faint cattle trail that angled southeast, toward the foothills of the Salts, and he turned down it. There were fresh deer tracks here, but nothing else, and he knew a savage impatience now. Why would John Evarts disappear? Not voluntarily. And the only men who knew of his sudden change of heart, his decision to fight, were Bide and Cavanaugh and their men.

But immediately he knew that was not right. The word would have got out, and any man in this country, acting on the theory that it was better to get rid of Evarts now than fight him later, could have ambushed him. Will turned his mind away from that possibility.

Presently the trail dipped down to skirt a small stream, and Will paused to let his horse drink. On the opposite bank he saw fresh tracks, and he roweled his horse over, a sudden excitement within him. And then it died. There were two pairs of tracks—one of a horseman, the other of a cow at a dead run. Some rider this morning had been pushing cattle out of the brush toward the flats.

Will put his horse around to drink again and took his feet out of the stirrups. Morosely he rolled a cigarette, idly listening to a pair of jays quarreling back in the timber. He was unable to conquer an obscure feeling of guilt within himself now, for he believed that somehow, in some way, John's disappearance was connected with his sudden change of heart there at the seep. And that affair was Will's doing. He lighted his smoke and absently held the match until it burned his fingers.

Afterward he pulled his horse away from the water and set off down the trail, wondering what he was going to tell Celia tonight. A man didn't vanish off the face of the earth and leave no sign, but how was he to explain that he couldn't find the sign?

In late afternoon he came to the edge of the timber and looked across the rolling country beyond, noticing without much surprise, that although this was Hatchet grass there were cattle on it.

And then his attention narrowed. Grazing among the cattle out there was a horse.

He put his own horse down on the flat among the cattle, who watched him curiously, and he did not even pause to identify their brand.

A hundred feet from the horse, the feeling of certainty came to him. This was John Evarts' chestnut gelding, and he had lost his saddle.

Riding closer, Will reined up, and a reluctant, cold dread was in him. This was what had been in the back of his mind all day. The chestnut stood there with his head up, looking incuriously at him. Will took bleak note of the direction the cattle had grazed, which was from the west. Somewhere off this side of the seep the horse had fallen in with the cattle.

The choice was here, and although Will already knew what he would do there was a certain formality in announcing it. He started off south now, headed for Boundary.

The town had taken up its evening life again, now that calf branding was over. In six years Will had learned the pattern well enough, so that, seeing the number of ponies ranked in front of the Belle Fourche were thinning out, he rode past them and turned the corner and pulled in at the courthouse on the side street. He tied his horse at the hitch rail and afterward he tramped across to Joe Kneen's office.

The courthouse was small and new, and Kneen's office was in a basement corner at ground level. It was dark now, but Will went inside and lighted the lamp and slacked into Kneen's chair, facing the locked desk. Though the building was new, this room contrived to seem used and already stale, and its floor was scummed with the tramped-in mud of the street.

Will was idly studying the reward dodgers on the wall when he heard footsteps approaching and came out of his chair.

Joe Kneen stepped in then and, seeing Will, he hauled up abruptly. Kneen's bony face was still, his eyes reflecting a sudden caution, and when Will nodded Kneen came on into the room, saying, "I wondered when you'd stop in to see me, Will."

"Did you? Why?"

Kneen's bland gambler's eyes regarded Will briefly, and then he shook his head. "I don't want to quarrel with you, Will, but there's nothing I can do. Phil took that range from Bide, and Bide took it back. It's open range, and the biggest man keeps it."

He went over to a chair in front of the desk and sat down.

Will drawled. "I got a hunch, Joe, you're going to be sorry you ever wanted to be sheriff."

"Why?" Kneen said sharply. "Is that a threat, Will?"

"Maybe." Will paused. "John Evarts hasn't shown up since yesterday. I found his horse this afternoon north of Russian Springs. Without a saddle."

Kneen's face came suddenly alert.

Will went on gently, "You better find him, Joe. I'll give you two days before I settle this my own way."

Kneen said sharply, "Now wait, Will!"

"Two days," Will repeated.

He wheeled and started out the door, and Kneen said, "Will." There was a mildness, a kind of resignation in his voice that checked Will and made him turn.

Kneen came out of his chair slowly and faced him, an earnestness about him that Will couldn't deny.

"Dammit, Will, I liked John Evarts."

Will relented a little. "That's all I know, Joe. He gathered up some of Ray Cavanaugh's stuff that was on our range yesterday and sent the boys back with it and he headed for Kennedy's place."

"Kennedy's?"

"I don't know why. Kennedy says he wasn't there. All sign is washed out. I rode through the hills this afternoon and came on his horse feeding with Bide's cattle."

Kneen chewed his lip nervously, staring at the doorway past Will. "Maybe he was set afoot or dragged."

"Do you think he was, Joe?"

Kneen shook his head and said quietly, "No."

Will waited. Kneen sighed and turned away. He walked down the room, and when he came back he paused before Will. "You likely thought a lot of things about me, Will. Did you ever believe I like murder, though?"

Will shook his head in negation.

"Then give a man a chance," Kneen pleaded. "Bide ain't a killer."

"Some of his friends are then."

Kneen made a loose, helpless gesture with his hand. "But two days ain't any time, Will."

Will's voice was almost cold, brutal. "You watched this build up, Joe. You could have stopped it any time, but you figured Hatchet might bluff down. It's too late for me to wait, Joe—way too late."

Kneen's eyes were bitter as he listened, and Will knew Kneen was already regretting his part in his. But Kneen had gambled that Hatchet would die without trouble, and Will had no pity for him. He said, "Two days," and stepped out into the night.

He put his horse into the main street, and now the thing that had been in the back of his mind since afternoon was immediate and distasteful. At home Celia would be waiting for this news, and he found a reluctance in himself to face her. It wasn't that she could blame him in any way, for she wouldn't; but to face her each night, seeing her hope die bit by bit, was what he hated. For he knew, without knowing why, that John Evarts wouldn't come back.

The smell of chill earth and wet wood was still in the spring air tonight, and it made Will oddly restless. He passed the Belle Fourche and across and up the street saw the lamp still burning in Priest's Emporium. Remembering with what tolerant humor the town accepted Lowell Priest's ceaseless and patient search for money, Will noticed that all the other stores were closed. Only Lottie's father, on the off-chance that some carousing ranch hand might remember his list and want accommodation, kept his store open at this hour. Thinking of Lottie now made him realize that she would not be moved by John Evarts' disappearance. She was outside of Hatchet, except where it touched him, and even then she did not understand his feeling for it.

Passing the store now, Will saw Priest seated at his desk in the balcony over the rear of the store. He reined up, suddenly struck by a thought that held him motionless a moment. Why should he go back to Hatchet and wait out these two days? The news of John's disappearance would serve to momentarily check the men who were moving in on Hatchet, while off in the hills somewhere was locked the mystery of where John Evarts had gone.

Will pulled over to the tie rail, dismounted, and went into Priest's store, his mind made up.

Priest, alert to the entrance of any customer, came down the stairs and approached Will between the neatly stacked counters. The smell of leather and cloth and kerosene was pleasant, and oddly Will thought of Priest as smelling of these same three staples.

Lottie's father was a thin, precise man with a sallow face that was polite and humorless. A thin pleasure was there now as he said, "You're riding late, Will."

"I want grub for a couple of days and a blanket," Will said. He followed Priest back to the grocery counter, and Priest said over his shoulder, "How're things at Hatchet?"

Will felt a faint annoyance, since Priest did not distinguish between the affairs of Hatchet and any other ranch. It was his stock greeting and held a wry humor at the moment which provoked Will into saying, "It's falling to pieces nicely, thanks."

Priest nodded absently and went about his business, and perhaps a minute later he straightened up. "What did you say, Will?" he asked blankly.

Will smiled and shook his head. "How's Lottie?"

"You're too late to see her," Priest said, a faint reproof in his voice. "She said something about wanting to see you."

"I'll be gone a couple of days."

Priest rounded up bacon and coffee and a small pot and pair of blankets. Will rolled his provisions into the blanket while Priest watched him, a mild disapproval in his eyes.

"You'll miss the dance Saturday," Priest said.

"So I will."

When he finished he glanced up to see Priest regarding him speculatively. "Will," Priest began, "I heard about a nice proposition this morning. A fellow wants someone to go in with him on shares running cattle."

"There's money in it," Will conceded, lifting his bedroll off the counter.

"A reliable fellow from over in the Indigos," Priest went on. "Wants to stock some new range quick."

Will looked swiftly at him, mention of the Indigos yanking him alert. The outfits in the

Indigos were safe friends of Hatchet, all of them.

"In the Indigos?" Will murmured.

Priest nodded, his face bland and watchful. "Like I said," Priest went on carefully, "it sounds like a nice proposition. This fellow says there's not much risk. I wondered what you thought."

A sudden wild anger smoldered in Will's eyes and then faded, and he drawled mildly, "If money's to be made there you might's well make some yourself, is that it?"

"That's what I figured."

Will murmured, "How big a risk do you think it is?"

"Not big," Priest said slowly. "How big do you?"

"Right now, not very big."

Priest smiled faintly. "Thank you, Will."

When Will had left Priest, smiling faintly with satisfaction, went up to his desk, drew out a piece of paper, and wrote a short note. He looked at the clock then, which said eleven. Rising, he put the note in his pocket and set about closing the store.

After locking the door he stepped out into the dark street and crossed it to the Belle Fourche.

Inside at the back there were a few scattered games of cards going on. Priest nodded gravely to the men standing at the bar and then paused and surveyed the cardplayers.

He saw the man he wanted, a hand from Harve Garretson's place out in the Indigos.

He went up to the players, interrupted the game long enough to give the note to Garretson's hand, and then left the Belle Fourche, nodding a grave good night to the bartender as he departed.

It had been a good day, a very good day, he reflected as he set out for home.

Chapter 6

The shock was still upon Joe Kneen as he rode out to Bib M next morning. He left the main road that skirted the Salt Hills a little after nine and took the wagon road lifting among the foothills to Bide Marriner's place. The breakfast he had bolted earlier was still heavy in his stomach, but that did not account entirely for the mild nausea he felt. John Evarts was probably dead, and this little scheme of Bide's that he had abetted, if not aided, was out of hand.

Kneen regretted bitterly that he had allowed things to come to this. John Evarts was too good a man to die alone in the brush at the hands of some riffraff from under Indian Ridge, and for that Kneen was genuinely sorry. Long ago, in moments of self-searching, Joe Kneen had read himself aright. He was a man born to work for other men, but only so long as his tolerant conscience approved. And it had never approved of murder.

Bib M, approaching it from this side, was a raw-looking place to Kneen. The L-shaped long house and porch squatted atop a low, bald knob barren of trees. Below it was an unlovely scattering of barns and corrals and sheds, a windmill thrusting its gaunt tower above them. It looked like a womanless place, Kneen thought, as he rode up to it.

Bide came out onto the porch in his shirt sleeves and put his shoulder against a porch post and watched Kneen climb the grade. He had found time to shave since roundup, and his swarthy face looked thinner, his black eyes brighter than ever.

He watched Kneen's gaunt, big-boned figure labor up the slope and he called, "Ride him up, Joe. That's what I do."

Kneen grunted as he came up and sat down on the edge of the porch.

"You're out early," Marriner said.

Kneen looked up at him, his pale eyes troubled. "Know anything about John Evarts, Bide?"

Bide grunted. "I found out I don't know anythin' about him. Why?"

"He's gone. They found his horse out

there above Russian Springs yesterday afternoon.

Bide looked at him blankly. "Gone? Where?"

"If you had a man disappear and his horse turned up without the saddle what would you think?"

Bide didn't answer for a moment, and then he said bluntly, "I'd think he was lyin' out in the brush somewhere with a shot in his back."

"I think that's where Evarts is."

Marriner stepped down off the low porch and sat beside Kneen. He scooped up a handful of gravel and sifted it slowly through his fingers and presently said without looking at Kneen, "That why you're out here?"

"Partly."

"I'm a damn fool, maybe, but not that kind of a one, Joe. You ought to know that."

"I do. But what about your men?"

"Go ask 'em. They're all out by Russian Springs except Russ. He left for Ten Mile this mornin'."

Kneen stared gloomily, out into the blue haze over the flats below, not knowing how to go about this and yet certain he should do something. He said gloomily, "Will Ballard will wait just two days before he cuts loose."

"On me," Bide said, and Kneen nodded. Bide said bitterly, "What about them little ten-cow outfits back under the Ridge?"

"Who put 'em onto Hatchet?" Kneen countered.

Marriner's dark eyes were hot now as he regarded Kneen. "Wait a minute," he said slowly. "Who told me to go ahead with this?"

"I didn't figure on murder," Kneen said grimly.

"You ain't, with me. I got nothin' to do with Evarts' disappearance, Joe, and I don't figure to. I got a job and I'm goin' to do it."

"You're going to stay put until I find Evarts," Kneen said flatly. He came to his feet now, and so did Marriner. Kneen topped Marriner by a head, and this fact alone seemed to anger Bide. He spoke hotly, arrogantly, "Joe, you try to stop me now and I'll run over you too."

"You'll stop until I find Evarts. I mean that, Bide." Kneen nodded curtly, and without speaking again he started down the hill.

"Joe! Joe!" Bide called.

Kneen halted and looked back at him.

"Whose man are you, Joe?" Bide called angrily. "I want to know."

"Why, damn you, Bide, I'm my own!" Kneen shouted.

He walked down to his horse and mounted without looking back. Marriner, his fury touched by a strange uneasiness, watched him go and knew the first faint stirrings of doubt.

From the timber on the slope off to the south Will also watched Kneen leave Bib M, and he could read nothing into the visit.

He pulled back into the timber and climbed behind Bide's place and then set off north along a rising trail toward Indian Ridge. His riding was almost aimless, but he kept to the ridges and paused now and then to watch the country. Below, on the flats, he saw a spring wagon cut across a corner of Sam's D Cross, headed toward the Springs. Farther west the sun flashed on a window of one of the shacks along Bandoleer Creek. Again he sought a trail, keeping to the high ground. Each trail he crossed he studied in silence, reading the movements of men and animals upon it.

That night he camped somewhere above

the junction of Indian Ridge with the Salt Hills, and next morning he was riding before daylight.

Now he was more alert, more careful, for this was the country under Indian Ridge. It was a rough country of tight-snarled valleys and sparse grass, and its ranches were small affairs run by men who coveted the good grass and sometimes the cattle to the south. Will was not loved in this country, and twice, when he heard riders approaching, he pulled off into the brush and let them pass. But he watched the trails and spent long hours observing one ranch and then another as he worked toward the Indigos. He watched Cavanaugh's small layout until he saw Cavanaugh himself drag out to the well for a bucket of water, a blanket wrapped around him. But nothing he saw during that day was out of the ordinary. He was not seen and he was not stopped, and he knew that if John Evarts was being held back in here it would be otherwise.

At dusk he drifted into the timber of the Indigos which lifted, tier on timbered tier, to the peaks and the reservation beyond.

He cut south then and picked up an old logging trail that slanted up the Indigos and presently, after dark, rode into the clearing that marked Ten Mile.

It was a shabby set of buildings on a bare stump-pocked valley floor flanking a rutted logging road that vanished up the canyon. There was the big saloon and, across the road, a store and blacksmith shop. Up the road was the unpainted hotel, converted from the logging-camp bunkhouse.

Will studied it from the darkness, and he knew this visit had been in the back of his mind when he set out from Boundary. He wanted to talk with Red Courteen.

It was early yet, and there were few horses at the saloon's tie rail. Will rode past the rusted skeleton of the abandoned mill boiler and past the saloon in the darkness and heard the conversation of two men on the porch break off abruptly. He noted, too, that one of the men immediately stepped into the saloon to spread the word of Will's presence.

Will dismounted at the store and went inside and bought some tobacco and afterward came out on the porch and rolled a cigarette. He smoked it completely, and afterward, figuring that Courteen had had time to get word of his presence, he cut across the rutted road and mounted the steps into the saloon.

Inside a pair of punchers were playing cards at one of the tables across from the bar, and they studiously avoided looking at him. In the back room two others were playing pool at the lone table, silent in feigned concentration. Will smiled faintly and walked up to the short bar and asked of the bartender, "Where's Red?"

The bartender tilted his head and said, "Inside."

Will tramped across to the door in the side wall at the head of the bar and turned to look at the cardplayers. He surprised them watching him, and he saluted them gravely before he opened the door and stepped inside.

The office was almost as big as the barroom, and in the far corner Red Courteen sat at his desk, his back to the door. He did not look up at Will's entrance, and Will waited a moment, watching him. When Courteen still did not look up Will opened the door and slammed it viciously.

The crash of its closing brought Courteen out of his chair to face Will.

"Don't do that to me, Red," Will murmured and started across the room.

Courteen sank back into his chair. He was a man of forty or so, and his thin, alert face held a toughness in it that was not spurious. His hair was kinky, a deep brick color, and fitted his narrow skull closely. There was a kind of sullen watchfulness in his green eyes as he regarded Will. They were dressed alike in waist overalls and calico shirt, except that Red wore a black coat as a badge of dignity.

Will looked around the room once and came to a halt by the table in the middle of the room, a big man whose arrogance had always baited Courteen's temper.

Red said thinly, "It took you longer than I figured, Will. You always get here, though."

"Don't I?" Will murmured.

Red nodded toward the door. "Go ahead. Look us over. Saloon, store, and hotel. Every room of it, if you want."

Will looked blankly at him, and only after a moment did understanding come. Courteen was talking about John Evarts, and Will was instantly alert. He said idly, "How'd you hear?"

"Kennedy rode through last night."

Will felt the sudden pulling of excitement, but his tone was casual as he asked, "Rode through? To where?"

Courteen shrugged. "Out of the country. He usually spooks first, don't he?"

Will said instantly, swiftly, "What did he say?"

Curiosity mounted into Courteen's eyes, and he didn't answer.

"What did he say?" Will asked sharply.

"Why, nothin', except you were on the prod lookin' for John Evarts. He got drunk too quick to talk much." He was frowning, puzzlement supplanting the dislike in his eyes.

Will stepped in front of him and said thinly, "Red, you better remember. Who'd he drink with? Who'd he talk to?"

Courteen came to his feet, saying slowly, "He's got a girl here. She works for me in the hotel, and he was with her. Why?"

"Take me to her."

Courteen shrugged and led the way out of the office and the barroom, and Will tramped silently beside him, his original business with Courteen forgotten now. For Kennedy had left the country, and Will knew it was not because he was afraid of having to pay Hatchet for a stolen cow. Kennedy knew something and he was afraid.

Crossing to the hotel in the darkness, Will remembered Kennedy's craven fear there at the shack, and he cursed himself silently and bitterly for having believed his story.

Courteen led him through the small lobby, past the desk, and into the dark dining room, where he paused, looking around. The dining room was a crude affair of deal tables and benches, and the dishes of half a dozen diners still remained uncleaned.

Courteen went past the tables toward the rear and shouldered through the door into the kitchen.

A middle-aged Indian woman was shoving wood into the stove, and she looked at them without interest. Beyond her at the crude sink stood a girl in a drab, faded dress, her back to them.

Courteen called, "Amelia," and the girl turned abruptly. She looked inquiringly at Courteen and then saw Will, and for a fleeting instant there was blank dismay in her face.

She knows, Will thought as Courteen said, "Will Ballard wants to talk to you."

Courteen left them, and the girl came slowly away from the sink, wiping her hands on a dirty apron. She was a plain drudge of a girl, Will saw, probably the only kind of woman Kennedy could attract. Her step was reluctant as he stepped back and held open the door into the dining room.

She walked through it and then faced him defiantly.

"Sit down," Will said gently.

The girl went over to a bench and seated herself, and she would not look at him. Her thin, unlovely face and work-reddened hands served to keep Will silent a moment. He was baffled as to how to begin this, for the girl, even in her silence, was already stubborn and unrelenting and somehow to be pitied.

Will said mildly, "What did Wes tell you about me, miss?"

"He didn't tell me anything," she flared. "I don't even know you."

She looked at him with a fierce resentment, and her glance fell away. Will knew a sudden discouragement, watching her. She would steadfastly deny knowing anything about Kennedy's affairs, and there was no way he could coax information out of her.

Will made his decision quickly, despising himself for it. He said in a normal voice, "Wes will have to ride pretty long and pretty far to get away from this murder charge, miss."

She looked at him now, and Will went on in the same tone, "John Evarts had friends all over the back coutry, a lot of friends."

"He didn't kill John Evarts!" the girl said defiantly.

"So Evarts is dead."

The girl saw her mistake immediately, and her face hardened. She started to rise, but Will put a hand on her shoulder and forced her gently back on the bench.

"I never thought Wes killed him," Will said. "What's the sense in him coming back to prove it?"

"He's gone! You can't bring him back. He never did anything!"

"He stole a Hatchet cow," Will reminded her.

"He didn't. He made that up!"

Will shook his head. "He admitted it to me and Jim Young. That's all Joe Kneen needs to send out his name to every county sheriff and have him brought back."

The girl was watching him now. Will went on, "What's the sense in hauling him back here to face that charge and maybe get a murder charge on top of it?" He paused and repeated, "What's the sense—when you can tell me all he knows."

"But I don't know anything!" She was close to tears, but Will went on implacably, "You know he didn't kill John Evarts, don't you?"

"Yes."

"Then how do you know? That's all I want from you, and I'll forget Wes."

The girl looked around the room and took a deep breath and then suddenly shook her head. "I can't tell you," she said, her voice almost a wail. "I've got to work here. If I told you I'd be killed too, maybe."

"Then why don't you follow Wes?" Will said quickly. "There's money to do it. I can give it to you."

She hesitated a long moment. "How much?" she whispered.

Will shrugged. "Whatever you like."

"A hundred dollars?" the girl asked defiantly.

Will nodded, feeling a pity for this girl.

"And—you'll give me time to get away?"

"As much as you want."

The girl looked down at her hands, and Will knew her courage was failing her. He said quickly, "You wait here and I'll get the money," and before she could protest he walked out of the dining room.

Courteen was standing on the edge of the porch smoking a cigar when Will came out and said, "I want to borrow a hundred dollars, Red. I want it now."

Red looked at him in the dark and said dryly, "Why should I give it to you?"

"Think a minute," Will murmured.

Red Courteen stared at him in the darkness, and his hatred was almost a tangible thing. Will knew what was keeping Red silent. It was the memory of Hatchet's vindictiveness. Red thought Hatchet would lose, but he wasn't sure enough of it to take the risk of crossing Will.

Courteen swore bitterly then and threw his cigar to the ground. It showered sparks as it struck, and Red said in a low, savage voice, "I'm not afraid of you, Will. Don't think that." Will said nothing; he knew he had won.

Red stepped off the porch then and headed for the saloon, and again Will fell in beside him.

They entered the barroom, and Will followed him into the office. In front of a squat, cast-iron safe in the corner Courteen knelt and, after a pause to work its combination, swung the door open and rose with a strongbox.

There was a faint, derisive smile on Will's face as Courteen counted out the gold eagles onto the table and shoved them across to him.

Courteen's hot glance raised to him now. "Phil Evarts told me once to stay off Hatchet. I'm telling you now. Stay out of Ten Mile, Will."

"I'll be back to pay you."

Courteen shook his head. "That hundred is to get you off my back. You better stay off."

Will picked up the coins and pocketed them and said, "I'll be back," and tramped to the door. He paused there and regarded Courteen and said with quiet arrogance, "When I come back, Red, you better sing soft."

He opened the door and stepped out, and he was immediately aware of the utter absence of talk, of any noise here. He closed the door behind him and looked around.

Russ Schultz stood at the end of the bar, his heavy, stupid face flushed with drink. At the table across the room were seated Ed

Germany and Hutch Williams, two ranchers from the Indigos who had always been friends with Hatchet. It could be one of these men with whom Priest had been talking of running cattle on shares. Marriner's man was here, talking to them tonight, and yet Will, seeing it, felt only a vast impatience to get back to the girl with the money.

He moved toward the door, and Schultz said loudly, "In a hurry, Will?"

"I am," Will answered calmly and walked out. Behind him as he went down the steps he heard the sudden murmur of voices, and he paid them no attention.

The girl was sitting in the dining room, just as he had left her. He went over to her and held out the handful of coins, and her hand slowly rose to take them.

"I shouldn't take these," she said uncertainly. "I don't really know."

"What is it?"

"Wes got too drunk," the girl said swiftly. "I took him to my room to sleep it off, but he kept talking."

Will watched her, patient.

"He was telling me he had to leave. I didn't know why. He kept telling me something else that I didn't understand." She paused, suddenly timid. "He kept saying, 'Ray shouldn't of shot him.' He said it over and over."

Will stood there, hardly breathing, and let this knowledge sink in. Cavanaugh, it was—and John had been shot to death. In swift reconstruction of it he saw that John had come to Kennedy's, and Cavanaugh had been there. They had quarreled, and Kennedy had seen it happen. Somehow Kennedy had decided to stay and face it out—maybe because he was afraid his absence would throw the blame on him—but his nerve had failed him in the end.

There was no anger in Will now, only a kind of wicked fatalism. He said, "How many days do you want?"

"I didn't understand it," the girl went on heedlessly. "Not until I heard the men talking at supper about John Evarts' disappearing." She looked at Will, and his face was bleak, uninterested. She said, "Two days, I guess," and Will nodded and went out.

He heard the quiet laughter of men on the saloon porch as he approached, and he shifted his gaze across the street to the tie rail in front of the store.

His horse was gone.

He hauled up, his attention arrested now. Again he heard the quiet laughter on the saloon porch and he thought he heard Schultz's voice along with Red Courteen's. With an effort of will, he put Ray Cavanaugh from his mind and forced himself into awareness.

He tried now to think back to when he left the saloon and of what he had only half heard Schultz say. Something about being in a hurry. And then it came to him. Schultz, remembering the bitter indignity of having to foot it home from the seep that day, was giving Will a taste of the same tough treatment. He was putting him afoot.

Seeing it, a welcome, reckless rage came to Will then, and he stood there tasting it in his mouth, feeling it take hold of him. For too many days he had been patient and accepting, seeing nothing he could get his hands on and hit. Now he knew John was murdered and something to hit was here, set up by this clumsy Schultz, and Will felt a hard and savage joy.

He stepped back farther from the road now and cut back into the deep darkness between the hotel and saloon. At the rear of the saloon he paused and softly opened the door. It let onto the back room, which was deserted now. Two billiard cues lay on the table among a scattering of balls.

Will softly stepped inside and moved forward, pausing by the table to look into the barroom. It was deserted, too, but standing in the swing doors, a hand on each one, pushing them out, stood Red Courteen. Red would enjoy this, Will thought wickedly.

His glance fell to the billiard table, and then he picked up three balls, cradling two of them in his left hand, holding the third in his right hand. He stepped clear of the table and threw.

The ball caught Red Courteen squarely in the back, and the wind was driven from him in a savage grunt as he pitched forward through the doors.

Will threw the second ball through the right-hand front window, shattering it in a jangle of glass. The third ball struck the window sill of the left window and caromed heavily through the glass into the darkness. A man outside howled curses, and then came the stampeding of feet as they all ran to get off the porch.

Will lifted his gun now and shot out the big overhead lamp. This left him with the pool-table lamp at his back, and someone outside, seeing him, let go a shot. It slammed into the ball rack on the rear wall, knocking it off its nail, and it crashed to the floor, spilling balls in all directions.

Will wheeled back against the wall and shot again, now at the lamp in the room. Its light was wiped out, and now he stood there, listening to the shouting outside, and smiled. Seeing a faint reflection of light from the bar mirror, he moved deeper into the barroom and picked up a chair and hurled it at the mirror. A series of crashes followed as the mirror collapsed into the stacked glasses which tumbled into the racked bottles and brought the whole upper works of the back bar down.

Will hurled another chair at Red Courteen's office door and then moved farther into the room, clinging to the wall.

He listened, and there was no sound from outside.

"Come on in, Red. Bring Schultz with you!" he yelled.

His answer was a fusillade of shots through both windows. He moved to a side window and kicked it out and stood by it, listening above the sound of the shots in front. Somebody pounded past the window on his way to the rear of the building.

Afterward Will slipped out the window, dropped to the ground, and moved toward the front of the building.

There was a man standing at the corner of it, flattened against the wall, and Will came up on him and put a hand on his shoulder and spun him around. It was Ed Germany, and when he saw Will he said quickly, "Hunh-unh. I'm not in this, Will."

Will stood by him and peered out into the street. From a corner of the blacksmith shop and from the far corner or the store men were shooting into the saloon.

Will said, "Your new friends aren't so tough, Ed," and he drifted into the darkness, moving far downstreet. When he was in complete darkness he crossed the road, and now he heard someone with a shotgun, probably the store clerk, blasting away at the rear door of the saloon. He came up the road now until he was a hundred feet from the blacksmith shop and on the same side of the street.

Fading into the darkness behind the old

mill boiler, he reloaded, watching the patient marksmen—two of them—at the corner of the blacksmith shop.

Now he stepped out and shot twice at the figures by the building and, turning, he ran behind the boiler and, still running, cut back of it, heading for the rear of the shop.

One man pounded past the rear corner, and Will collided with the second as they both ran for the corner. Will put a hand on his back and shoved viciously, and the runner sprawled off into the darkness, and Will heard him crash among the stacked scrap iron beyond the back wall of the shop.

Rounding the corner now, Will saw Schultz paused by a window in the store's rear, feverishly loading his gun. Will shot once and he saw Schultz half turn to look and then, panic on him, drive for the store's rear door.

He had it half open when Will hit, crashing it shut. He caromed off it into Schultz, and they both went down. Will fell into the woodpile away from Schultz, who scrambled to his feet. Will slipped once getting up and shot again at Schultz, who was running blindly along the rear of the faintly lighted store building.

And then Will, running again now, heard a crash and the shriek of rending boards, and above that the wild cursing of Schultz. He hauled up, seeing Schultz on the ground. Bide's foreman, in his panic, had run full tilt into the shed forming the L at the rear of the store.

Schultz yelled wildly, "Don't, Will!"

He staggered heavily to his feet now and moved into the dim light cast through the rear window of the store. Beyond them, out in the street, the shooting continued with the same senseless vehemence.

Schultz had his hands shoulders high, and one leg of his overalls was ripped almost off and was dragging. A jagged gash in his leg was bleeding, and his heavy face now was distorted with his deep, heavy breathing.

Will, breathing heavily, too, said, "Where's my horse, Russ?"

"In the blacksmith shop," Schultz panted.

Will waited until his breath eased, and then he said, "Russ, you tell Bide I'm through waiting. Tell him that."

He left Schultz and went back to the blacksmith shop and pulled open the doors. The shooting in the street was muffled in here, and Will led his horse out into the night and mounted.

He put him behind the old boiler and then, reining up in the street, he called, "Red! Red Courteen!"

The shooting slacked off and Will yelled, "I'll be back and pay you, Red!"

Almost at once the shooting was resumed, and this time in his direction. He rode off down the road, listening, and above the hammering din of the shooting he heard Red Courteen's wild cursing.

Chapter 7

Ike Adams was not in a loving mood as he rode toward Hatchet this afternoon. This morning his last two real cow hands had quit. They were certain that the disappearance of John Evarts was the start of the bitter fight, and they didn't want any of it. They refused to wait for Will even, directing that their pay be mailed them. That left Hatchet with Ike, the cook, and the two rawhiders. Ike was bitter about the Young brothers. Hatchet's reputation was something dear to Ike, and he did not like to see it placed in the care of a couple of broke, thieving saddle bums who were rawhiders in the bargain. Proof of their shiftlessness, if further proof were needed, had been presented to Ike this morning.

On leaving Hatchet he had directed them to ride a piece of the west boundary and meet him at a spot on the north range, where Ike expected another of the Indian Ridge trash would have run in some cattle. The cattle hadn't been there, and no trouble occurred, but the defections of the Young boys galled him. On the way back he had occupied his time with framing a blistering report on them to Will.

He came into Hatchet through the low hills to the north and skirted the house, and only when he was in the clear did he see the knot of horses and men down by the corral.

He put spurs to his horse and, approaching closer, saw Harve Garretson from up in the Indigos. He was dismounted and he was talking vehemently to the two rawhiders. They were lounging lazily against the corral gate, listening idly, while a mounted man, a hand of Garretson's, watched.

As Ike rode up the Young boys glanced over at him, and Garretson, seeing them look, turned in Ike's direction. Garretson was a colorless, nondescript man of middle age who had a reputation of being a shrewd trader and minding his own business. He was dressed in a black suit, and his roan mustaches were so full they gave him a lugubrious air.

When he saw Ike he gestured wildly,

pointing to the horse pasture, and said angrily, "Ike, I've got a hundred head of cattle in there and I want 'em back!"

Ike looked sharply at the Young boys. Mel had a boot heel hooked over one of the gate poles, and his battered Stetson was shoved back of his forehead. He was chewing idly on a hay straw and when he looked at Ike his eyes were mild, innocent.

"What's this?" Ike demanded.

"You told us to watch out for any strange beef this side of the line, didn't you?"

Ike looked at Garretson and said cautiously, "Some of your stuff stray over, Harve?"

"Five miles over," Jim Young drawled. He was squatted by Mel, and his eyes also were innocent, Ike noticed.

Garretson said angrily, "I'll give you a chance to return 'em Ike, and I'll forget to tell Will about this."

Ike, up to now, had been faintly embarrasse, remembering that Garretson, like all the outfits in the Indigos, had been good neighbors to Hatchet. But Ike didn't like threats, and after considering this a moment he decided it was a threat.

He said, "I'll tell him myself. How far over the line was your stuff?"

"Five miles," Jim Young repeated.

Ike said flatly, "I'm askin' him," to Jim Young.

Mel said, "Jim just wanted to be sure you heard right."

Ike, nettled, turned back to Garretson. "That right?"

Garretson came over to him and put a hand on Ike's horse, and now his voice was confidential. "That's right, Ike. Only let's get some sense into this talk."

Ike didn't say anything, and Garretson went on persuasively, "You know and I know that Will and John Evarts don't aim to try and keep all of old Hatchet. They can't. Well, these cattle"—he gestured toward the horse pasture—"are my claim to that chunk that borders on me. That's only reasonable, ain't it?"

"You're pretty sure," Ike drawled ominously.

"Sure?" Garretson laughed easily. "Know who's part owner of them cattle with me, Ike? Lowell Priest."

Ike was startled. The whole country knew that Will was going to marry Lottie Priest someday. Certainly Priest wouldn't allow his cattle to be driven onto Hatchet, risking seizure, unless Will had given the word to go ahead. But Will hadn't said anything to him, and that was enough for Ike.

He said, "Mebbeso. I'll ask him."

"That's right," Garretson said, and he turned to the Young brothers. "I told you fellows this was Priest's herd. Now help me cut 'em out!"

"They'll keep right here," Ike said.

Garretson turned on him. "You mean you're goin' to hold 'em anyway?"

"Till Will says to drive 'em back, I am."

Garretson stood there, speechless with anger. Jim Young rose and handed him two six-guns and drawled mildly, "We'll let you know what he says."

Garretson took the two guns, gave one to his man, who had watched this with utter indifference, and tramped over to his own horse. He stepped into the saddle and pulled his horse around, facing Ike.

"You'll be damn sorry for this, Ike!" he shouted, shaking his fist. "The whole scummy crew of you will get your time for this!"

"Good-by, Mr. Garretson," Ike said dryly.

Garretson roweled his horse, and his

puncher fell in beside him, and they rode rapidly down the fence line.

Ike looked over at the herd in the horse pasture. Garretson's bunch had been the biggest catch yet. The grass was nearly gone in the pasture, and Ike didn't have any idea what Will was going to do with all the captive cattle, but it was at least tangible evidence that Hatchet was fighting. He looked now at the Youngs.

Mel said, "We kind of figured we already had this bunch, and we didn't have that other bunch you was talkin' about, so we brought 'em in."

"Any trouble?"

"One fella argued. We didn't bring him along."

Ike grinned then, and surprisingly the Young brothers grinned back at him.

"Maybe," Ike said in a dry, dubious voice, "you'll make Hatchet hands yet."

Chapter 8

It was the following afternoon that Celia heard the door into the office close and she said, "Wait, Sam," and went into the corridor. Paused there, she listened, head tilted and looking absently at Sam, who had ceased his pacing in the exact center of the pattern on the living-room carpet.

She heard movement in the office and started hurriedly down the corridor. Halfway, the office door opened and Will started through it and then, seeing her, he stopped and stepped back into the office.

Celia came forward slowly, a kind of dread holding her back. She first saw the somber ugliness in Will's deep-set eyes, the tough, unforgiving set of his lean jaw, and she knew.

She said, "John's dead," and Will nodded.

Sam tramped heavily down the corridor

and came into the room and said, "What? What's that, Will?"

"Cavanaugh shot him."

Sam looked skeptical. "How do you know?"

Briefly Will told of what had passed at Ten Mile and of what the girl had told him.

Celia only half listened to him. She was gauging the depth of Will's temper now, listening to his quiet, unemotional words, and she detected in them a reluctance to talk about this. In herself she strangely felt nothing, and she knew it was because she had expected it, was certain it would happen. In her own mind she had been grieving for John Evarts these past three days, and she knew that Will had too. It was Sam who was shocked, whose slow mind turned over these facts uncomprehendingly, really only half believing them.

As Will concluded he was looking at her, talking to her, and she had a fleeting glimpse of his anger. He would be as implacable as an Indian now, and Celia, seeing this, was afraid.

Will said to her, "Hatchet's yours now, Celia," and walked over to the desk.

She didn't say anything, and Will turned

and looked searchingly at her. Then his glance dropped and he said quietly, "I'm quitting." His glance raised quickly again, holding hers, searching for understanding.

I've got to be careful, Celia thought, and she said nothing. She walked over to the worn sofa and sat on it, hearing Sam say, "There's nothing more you can do, Will," in an unctuous tone of voice that she hated.

Will didn't look at Sam, didn't answer him. He came out into the middle of the room, facing her, his big shoulders a little stooped, and he was waiting for her answer.

Celia understood instinctively that a choice was here and that it would be irrevocable. Will was going to kill a man, and he did not want her to share the blame. If she was silent Will would ride off Hatchet and never blame her for her decision, and she knew deep within her that she would not let him go. He was a part of her and a part of her life. If she had liked that in him which she had seen each day these past six years then she must like this, because this was Will Ballard too. Nothing mattered now, except that she must take the ugly with the fine. And even now, Will was generous; he was trying to free her of any responsibility.

Only a corner of her mind acknowledged Sam Danfelser as she said, "I'll stand by you, Will."

Will said, "Celia, I——"

"I know," Celia said quickly. "If it's what you have to do, Will, then do it. I'll stand by you."

Sam looked in puzzlement from one to the other, not understanding this. Neither of them was including him, and he said in flat protest, "Celia, what are you talking about?"

Will looked at him and said, "Cavanaugh."

Sam didn't even understand then for a long moment, but when he did the alarm in his eyes was immediate.

"Now wait, Will," he began.

Will said flatly, harshly, "Cavanaugh killed John," and he turned and left the room.

Celia didn't watch him; she tucked one foot under her and was aware that Sam's outraged glance was on her. He came over to her and said, as if he were talking to a child, "But he's going to kill Cavanaugh."

"I know." Celia's slim face held a sadness he did not see.

"But Celia!" Sam said harshly. "That's murder!"

Celia shook her head. "No, Sam. That's less than murder for murder, and you know it."

She rose and brushed past him, and Sam put out his hand and took her elbow. She didn't fight against him; she let him turn her around to face him, and she was not even angry. She was thinking bitterly, *Poor Will*.

Sam said accusingly, "You let him go."

"Dad trusted Will. I do too."

Sam shook her roughly in his impatience. "But don't you understand? He's going out to murder a man, and you let him go!"

"Let me go, Sam," Celia said quietly.

Sam looked down at his hand which was grasping her arm tightly, and then he let go of her. He shook his head from side to side almost like a man in pain. "But, Celia, we have laws; we have a sheriff; we have a jail; we have a judge; we can get a jury. Try the man. Don't kill him!"

Celia responded, "This is Will's affair."

"But you wouldn't let him quit Hatchet! You asked him to stay on, knowing where he was going. You're to blame as much as he

"And I'm willing to take it."

Sam was baffled. There was a terrible urgency in his face, in his eyes, and Celia felt a momentary pity for him. He was like a man who suddenly discovers among friends that his language is unaccountably not understood by them.

She said quietly, "Sam, there's so much you don't understand. There's lots I don't, too, but I understand the way Will feels now. Don't you see? Hatchet's on trial. Will we revenge our own or will we take this to a lawyer and watch him argue in a courtroom in front of all those people who hate us and hold us in contempt?" She shook her head, her eyes pleading. "Don't you see that Will can't do it, Sam? Right or wrong, he's got to do it this way."

Sam spoke with a thick fury in his voice. "You talk like a drunken squaw!"

"I guess I do," Celia said quietly, miserably—and stubbornly.

They stood there facing each other, neither speaking, Sam solid and implacable and filled with a righteous fury. Celia seemed even smaller than usual now in her meekness. But she did not go to him; she faced him, reading angry, unspoken thoughts in his ruddy face.

Sam groaned softly. "Why, Celia?" he pleaded softly. "Why?" His eyes were questioning, too, and Celia would rather have faced his anger.

"It's just the way I am, Sam," she answered quietly.

Sam hesitated a moment, and a slow, shrinking distaste came into his face as he said, "Are you in love with Will?"

"I'm going to marry you, Sam," Celia said quietly.

"He's done something to you," Sam said slowly, wrathfully. "He's changed you into something—something I can't put a name to—until now you can tell him to go out and kill a man, and it doesn't do anything to you."

Celia was silent, accepting this. Everything Sam said was true, and yet she felt no guilt and she wondered why.

Sam turned away from her as if to go out, and then he paused and came back. "Celia," he said grimly, "you're going to get rid of Will."

There was a fleeting protest in Celia's gray eyes, and she did not answer.

Sam started for the door again, and Celia said, "Where are you going, Sam?"

"To tell him he's through with Hatchet."

"But he isn't," Celia said quietly. "You can tell him, but he won't believe you."

There was a pride in her now as she went on back into the corridor, leaving Sam alone.

He stood there scowling at the door and then went after her. Turning into the living room, he walked across to the sofa where his hat lay. He picked it up and stepped out into the late-afternoon sun and headed for the corral where he had turned his horse in.

Jim Young, watching him from the bunkhouse steps, drifted down to the corral after him. Ike, since the brush with Garretson yesterday, had left him at the ranch to keep watch over the captive herd in the horse pasture.

He held open the gate for Sam, who did not even bother to nod his thanks. Jim watched him head out north, taking the same trail Will had taken before him.

Paused at the gate, Jim Young considered. He could read murder in a man's eyes, and he had read it in this heavy man's face, just as he had read it in Will's face a half-hour ago, both when he went into the house and came out. Will hadn't even spoken to him, but Jim knew.

There was a moment of indecision as he watched Sam's stocky horse disappear beyond the house. Then, with only a faint stirring of conscience, Jim reached for his rope on the gatepost and stepped inside the corral to catch his horse.

There was not a light in Cavanaugh's place. Will made sure of that before he drifted down the timbered slope in the darkness sometime after midnight and came into the hard-packed yard in front of the mean shack that lay deep and remote in the Ridge country.

At the well he paused to listen and, hearing nothing, he went on up to the porch and halted in front of the door. He drew his gun then and kicked the door open and stepped aside and said, "Come out, Cavanaugh!"

There was no answer. He waited, hearing nothing but his own soft breathing, and presently he slipped inside, clinging to the wall. Still he heard nothing. Fumbling in his shirt pocket, he brought out a match and wiped it alight on one of the wall logs. The shabby interior of Ray Cavanaugh's one room house came into sudden focus now. The bunk in the back corner was empty.

Dirty dishes littered the table, and there was a pot on the stove next the end wall.

The match died, and Will moved over to the stove and put his hand on it and found it cold.

He stood there in the dark a moment, debating, and then, his judgment given, he went over to the bunk and lay down on it. He put his gun beside him, pillowed his head on his arms, and watched the door. He was going to wait, certain that Cavanaugh would return sometime.

Lying there in the dark, he put his mind to what would happen afterward, and moments later discovered that he was thinking not of that but of Celia. He saw her as he had left her, sitting on the sofa, a foot tucked under the worn dress that Sam Danfelser had doubtless surprised her in. She had not failed him; she was Phil Evarts' girl. Somberly Will pondered what that meant for her, and he knew her decision had been bitter. Sam Danfelser, like a hulking, obstinate bear, was to be faced afterward, and that would not be easy for her. Will had tried to help her in a thousand things, large and small, but he could not help her with Sam. She had never asked for any help, never spoken a disloyal word of Sam, but, nonetheless, Will sensed things were not right between them. He thought bleakly of Sam Danfelser then and knew that when Celia and Sam married it would be time for him to leave Hatchet. That would please Lottie.

He shifted his weight on the bunk and had a sudden hunger for a cigarette. Slowly, though, his thinking reverted to Lottie again, and he was faintly troubled. She had never liked his remaining at Hatchet, and now what would she think in the face of this turn of events? What would she think of him here, now, tonight, waiting patiently to kill a man?

He put this instantly from his mind and sat up. He fumbled in the dark for his tobacco and fashioned a cigarette and put it in his mouth. Match in hand, he was weighing the risk of having the smell of tobacco linger in this room to give his presence away against the hunger pulling at his nerves. And then he heard it.

A horse was being ridden into the yard.

He balled up the cigarette and discarded it, coming silently to his feet. Moving away from the bunk, he held his gun at his side and waited, listening, his nerves pulling taut.

He heard the rider dismount, heard his step on earth and then on the porch, and now a figure darkened the opening of the doorway.

Gun at side, he waited, and then came the simultaneous scratch of a match and its light.

Sam Danfelser stood just inside the door, match held over his head, peering through squinted lids at Will.

Will let his breath go and didn't move.

Sam said contemptuously, "Is that the way it's done? Catch him in the dark?"

He moved heavily over to the table and lifted the chimney from the lamp and lighted the wick, and then his gaze lifted to Will, who hadn't moved.

Will's eyes glittered darkly as he watched Sam, and he was impatient and curious and disgusted.

Sam said, "We've got to talk, Will."

"Later," Will murmured.

"No. Now."

Will said with rising intolerance, "I've got something to do, Sam. You're in the way. Get out."

"I'll get out when I've finished. It's time we talked."

Behind his obstinacy Will detected a note of urgency in Sam's voice, in his face, and he felt a small start of curiosity. "What do you want, Sam?"

"You're through at Hatchet." Sam's voice was flat, final. He stood by the table, solid and thick-bodied, and in his ruddy face was the expression of a man who had been pushed beyond the limit of patience. He could not have hidden the hatred for Will in his eyes if he had cared to, and he did not. Will saw this, and a startled caution was in him. For an instant he tried to understand Sam's anger and he could not, and the effort vanished in the dark narrow framing of a question.

"Did Celia send you?"

"I came for myself. I say you're through with Hatchet. You're not going back."

With calculated insult Will said, "You're ahead of yourself, Sam. Hatchet isn't yours to boss yet."

Sam came around the table and halted, and his face was ugly. "She's done with you, I say. You've turned her into a silly fool with your damned reckless talk. You've killed her uncle and you've turned her against me. Get out—while you're still alive."

Will felt his belly harden and the muscles in his chest grow taut. Sam stood with feet apart, one hand grasping the edge of the table, and his lips were white with anger.

Will said soberly, "You can bully women, Sam. Keep to them and don't bother with me."

Sam lunged for him then. Will dropped his gun and came at him at the same instant, so that their movements seemed almost prearranged. They met with an impact that drove their breaths from them, and Sam wrapped his thick arms around Will as if to crush him. Wordlessly, their feet scuffling on the dirt floor for bracing, they wrestled for long seconds, Sam trying to crush Will, and Will trying to break the hold. And then Sam's grip broke and Will came away, his fist lashing out to clout Sam on the ear.

Again Sam rushed, but this time Will met him with a driving blow in the mouth. Sam shook his head and started to slug, and they stood toe to toe, trading loping, hurting blows, both men silent except for grunts of savage exertion. Will felt a murderous exaltation, a kind of maniac lust to crush and smash this man. All the contempt for Sam, the thousand dislikes that he had kept to himself because of Celia now burst in his mind like water pouring over a dam.

They were hurting each other. Sam winced as his blow caught Will on the head, and he felt the shock of it in his shoulder. He gave a low, snarling cry and lowered his head and came at Will. His head caught Will in the chest and staggered him back against the wall. Will was brought up with a jarring thud that shook the walls, and then Sam, following his advantage, drove his head again into Will's midriff.

The impact drove the breath from Will. He pumped wild, flailing blows at Sam's head, and then his knees buckled and he fell forward on all fours.

Head down, gagging for breath, he was on his hands and knees when he felt the savage kick in his side. The force of it rolled him over and brought him joltingly against the bunk.

He saw Sam coming at him again now and he rolled out of the way and came to his feet and caught a looping blow on the head that sent him down again. But the pain of it seemed to clear his head.

He saw Sam standing by the table, feet planted wide apart, the coat torn off him, his face smeared with blood and agonized with the effort to get his breath. Will came up and at him then, driving into him with his shoulder and digging in his feet as he wrapped his arms around Sam and heaved.

Sam clawed at his back, off balance, and then he left the ground and was thrown across the bunk. His heavy body landed angling astride it, and there was a sound as sharp as a gunshot as the dry pole splintered and broke. The whole frame collapsed under his weight. Sam's head was brought sharply against the wall logs, and he half sat, half lay among the shattered poles of the bunk, shaking his head to clear it, already fighting to get up.

Behind his terrible concentration Will saw the shadows of the room change shape and then forgot it as Sam came at him.

Jim Young, who had followed Sam and only now had come into the room, moved quickly across it behind Will to lift the lamp from the table and retreat to the door, holding it shoulder-high to light the room.

Will met Sam's charge with his body half

turned, riding the drive of it, and together they stumbled into the table, overturning it against the wall before they fell across it.

Will, close to Sam now, slugged drunkenly and blindly at Sam's face. He was dragging great shuddering gasps of air into his tortured lungs now. Sam rolled over and came to his knees and then to his feet, Will rising with him.

Will lashed out and missed and fell into Sam, and Sam swung weakly at his head, shoving him away from him.

Will weaved back on his heels and came in again, and now Sam's arms were too tired to lift in defense. His head turned with Will's raking, tearing blow, and when he faced Will again the mark of bloody knuckles lay across his face.

Again Will came at him, stumbling, and Sam, eyes glazed, gave ground, bowing his head and swinging wildly, aimlessly. Implacably, barely on his feet, Will came at him still, hitting him again and again, and when he missed he would fall against Sam and steady himself and lash out again. Behind bruised cheekbones Sam's eyes were glazed, but in them burned a hatred that chilled Jim Young as he watched from the door.

The two of them leaned against each other a moment, gathering strength, and then Will lashed out again. The blow caught Sam in the throat, and he staggered back until he was brought up against the stove.

Doggedly and implacably, every breath rattling in his throat, Will stumbled into him again, swinging wide, tired blows.

Sam made one last stand, bracing himself and swinging his heavy fists with a dragging, terrible weariness. But one of Will's blows broke through his guard and pushed, rather than drove, him off balance. He crashed into the stove, overturning it, bringing down the pipe with a booming racket. Somehow he managed to keep his feet, and Will fell into him, slugging again with slow, grunting viciousness. The weight of him bowled Sam over. He fell across the stovepipe, landing heavily on his back, then rolled over on his side, face to the wall, and did not move.

Will, on his belly among the sooty dust of the pipe, came to his hands and knees now and crawled toward Sam.

Jim Young put the lamp down on the sill and came over to him and put a hand under his arm, and Will shook him off weakly, still crawling toward Sam.

"He ain't fightin' any more, Will," Jim said.

Again he put a hand under Will's arm, and this time Will didn't fight him. He came to his feet, weaving drunkenly, and Jim pushed his back against the wall and propped him there while Will, head hung in utter exhaustion, breathed in great whistling gusts of precious air.

Presently, when his breath came easier, he raised his head. A corner of his mouth was bloody and swollen where one of Sam's blows had mashed a lip against his teeth. One cheekbone was cut, and so was an eyebrow. His shirt was in ribbons, and on the pale skin of his chest were deep, livid bruises and welts. He raised his hands and looked at his raw and bloody knuckles, and then he moved weakly down the wall to look at Sam.

Jim Young watched him, silent, a little afraid.

Will reached out a foot and rolled Sam on his back. His eyes were closed; there was a faint bubbling sound in his bloodied nose as he breathed.

Will looked stupidly at Jim Young then. "How'd you get here?"

"Followed him."

Will said, "Get my gun over there and come into town with me."

Up on the timbered slope above the shack Ray Cavanaugh watched the scene in the yard below. Approaching his place from the Ridge trail moments ago, he had seen the lamplight and had pulled his horse off in the brush and circled wide to reach this spot. He watched now with a breathless concentration as a man he did not know came out of the shack below, put the lamp on the edge of the porch, and went back to the door.

Then Will Ballard came out, declining the offer of help from the other man, and walked slowly to his horse.

Cavanaugh had seen enough. He went quietly back to his horse and stood there in the dark, breathing softly. Will Ballard knew. A thin, dismal fear plucked at Cavanaugh as he acknowledged this. He knew he would be hunted tirelessly and implacably, maybe for a week, maybe for months, but in the end he would have to face Will Ballard.

His mind worked now with a slow, sly cunning, for in the dark hours since that day in the rain at Kennedy's he had had time to plan for this. Kennedy was gone, the only witness to the truth. If he framed his story rightly and admitted the killing he could claim the protection of the only man strong enough to fight Will Ballard. He mounted and set off through the timber for Bide Marriner's Bib M.

Chapter 9

Lottie finished her lonely breakfast and carried the dishes from her and her father's breakfast from the table in the kitchen to the sink. She bought out the tin dishpan and sloshed boiling water in it from the kettle on the stove. At the pump by the sink she tempered the water, then rolled up her sleeves. She paused for a moment, frowning, then sighed gently.

This was comfortable ritual, which she usually enjoyed, but this morning things were wrong. The news her father had given her at breakfast was disturbing. She rarely saw her father angry, but he had been angry this morning. He had told her, with a biting sense of injustice, the news brought to him from Garretson's late last night. His and Garretson's cattle had been seized by Hatchet.

And Will was not here to explain or to question.

She hurried through the dishwashing, looked at the clock, and was in the act of taking off her apron when she heard the knock on the door.

She crossed the room and opened it and stepped back, smothering an exclamation.

Will stepped into the room and closed the door behind him.

"Oh, Will, what's happened?" Lottie breathed.

"Nothing that won't wash off," Will said mildly. He crossed to the sink and began pumping water in a basin, and Lottie came up beside him.

Will looked at her and said, "Danfelser."

"But you and Sam——" Her voice faded away.

"There's lots you don't understand," Will said gently. "Clear out while I clean up, and dig me out a shirt of your father's. I'll tell you afterward."

Lottie, after some searching, found a shirt big enough for him, and when she came back Will, stripped to the waist, was bending down in front of the mirror, combing out his snarled black hair.

He took the shirt and shrugged into it, looking somberly at Lottie. "Cavanaugh killed John Evarts," he said. In short, plain words he told of what had passed at Ten Mile and finally at Cavanaugh's and all the while he was trying to button the shirt. His swollen fingers were too clumsy, however, and Lottie did it for him, listening to the grisly finish of his account.

Her eyes were dark with pain as she lifted one of his hands and looked at his raw, swollen knuckles.

"Will, what's going to happen?" she asked suddenly.

"I'm going to be busy," Will answered evasively.

"Will, look at me," Lottie said sharply.

Will turned dark, sullen eyes on her, and she said, "But you're through. Don't you see that? Hatchet is Sam Danfelser's worry now, and you've fought with him. You're out of it—forced out of it, at last."

"I don't see it, no." Will looked at her, his eyes still sullen.

"What will Celia do when she hears of your fight?" Lottie asked swiftly. "Do you think she'll side with you against the man she'll marry?"

Will couldn't answer her, and Lottie came close to him and put both hands on his chest. "Will, I haven't asked for much. I want to ask it now, though. Leave Hatchet. Pull out of that snarling pack of dogs and let's make a life for ourselves—another life besides Hatchet's."

"But I can't pull out."

"You can!" Lottie said passionately. "All along your loyalty is all that's held you—loyalty to John Evarts and to Celia. John's dead now. Hatchet's Celia's, and she's going to marry a man who'll take over for her. This is the time to quit, Will. You've got to!"

Will shook his head. "Sam can't handle it. Celia doesn't want him to. I offered to quit, and she wanted me to stay."

Lottie's face altered a little, but Will did not notice that. He said softly, bitterly, "I don't even want to quit, Lottie."

"Why?"

Will shook his head, watching her. "Red Courteen and Bide Marriner and Joe Kneen. Sam Danfelser and Cavanaugh and all the others. I don't know. I can't explain it, Lottie."

"They're all pulling you in," Lottie said

slowly, her voice almost hard. "I'm trying to pull you out. I don't matter that much, Will?"

"That's different," Will said impatiently.

"It's your pride, you mean," Lottie said, and she was angry now, angry enough to take advantage of his inarticulate, clumsy arguments. For it had come to Lottie now that her happiness was at stake, and she was fighting for it, womanwise. She said, gibingly, "See what it's done for you, Will? It's made people hate you so much they want to kill you. It's brought you between a girl and her man. It's kept me dreading to hear a knock on the door for fear it'll be news that you've been shot." She was fighting now, and out of the depths of her need to convince him she blurted, "It's even made you dishonest, Will."

Will had taken all this, smarting under its hurt, but at this last accusation protest flared in his eyes. Lottie, seeing it, said defiantly, "You told Dad to put his money into cattle you later took from him—on a whim of your pride."

"When was this?" Will asked slowly.

"Didn't you know? Your men seized the herd—after you'd told Dad it was safe to go in on shares with Garretson!"

The thin tenuous thread of Will's patience snapped now, and he spoke with a cold, reckless anger. "Your father has his damned greed to thank for that, Lottie."

This bald, flat statement held Lottie speechless with surprise, and it sobered her. It sobered Will, too, and they regarded each other carefully, each aware of the danger of further talk. But Lottie's pride had been hurt now and would not let her keep silent. "You deny you encouraged Dad to help Garretson stock his new range?"

"Lottie, Lottie," will chided gently. "Whose range? Hatchet's range? Would I do that?"

"He said you did."

"He asked in that damned sly way of his if there was a risk in moving in. I left it to him. He could read anything into that he wanted, and he did."

"And his cattle were seized by your men," Lottie said accusingly.

Will nodded. "They'll stay seized too."

They faced each other, both knowing there was nothing more to say unless one of them acknowledged wrong. Lottie's new independence was bolstered by the feeling that her father had been made to seem a shabby liar, and her loyalty would not allow her to apologize. Will, knowing he was in the right, was just as stubborn.

It was Lottie who turned to look at the clock and say quietly, tonelessly, "I'll be late for school, Will. I have to go."

Will moved to the door and opened it, then paused, looking back at her. She would not look at him, and he said, "Good-by, Lottie," and stepped out.

The thin cold sunlight didn't seem to warm Will as he stepped stiffly into the saddle and rode downstreet. The stores were just opening up, their clerks calling back and forth across the street, some of them sweeping the plank walk in front of their places of business. Will rode past them, unseeing, his thoughts troubled and ugly.

In front of Priest's Emporium he reined up and looked at the building, a gray dislike in his face. The thought that in the midst of all this trouble he would let Lowell Priest's affairs intrude filled him with a harsh contempt of himself, and he rode on. Crossing the four corners, he saw something that made him halt. Celia's black mare was tied in front of the Stockman's House. He regarded it a moment, the aching weariness of his legs and the smarting of his swollen lip reminding him of Sam Danfelser. There was Celia to face too.

He pulled in beside the black and dismounted and tramped into the lobby of the Stockman's House.

Celia was standing in front of one of the leather chairs in the lounge. Her gray riding habit was the same color as her eyes, Will noticed idly, and he went across the lobby to her.

Celia saw first the marks of the fight, and then she looked searchingly into his eyes, trying to read the story of what had happened since he'd left Hatchet. She could not, and yet she knew that whatever had happened he was here beside her, safe.

Will paused beside her and asked quietly, "Have you seen Sam?"

Celia shook her head.

"He followed me to Cavanaugh's last night. He wanted me to leave Hatchet."

Celia said slowly, "You fought with him," and when Will nodded she asked, "What about Cavanaugh?"

"I missed him."

Celia didn't say anything, and Will

watched her with humble curiosity. Presently he murmured, "I'm sorry it had to happen this way, Celia."

"Sam, you mean." She smiled faintly, almost sadly. "Sam always means what he says. He never thinks anybody else means what they say, Will. It's all right."

Will felt a weight lifted from him, and he knew this was the end of it. Celia still wanted him at Hatchet, and he still wanted to be there. He said, "Have you told Kneen?"

"I wanted to let you tell him."

"We'll both go," Will said.

They went out and downstreet and, walking beside Celia, it occurred to Will for the first time that at Hatchet things would be like they had been when Phil was alive. Out of this trouble had come one thing; he alone was responsible for Hatchet now. It wasn't an uncertain old man any more; it was himself—because Celia's wisdom or her mistakes were his own. It came to him, too, that these happenings had changed her already, putting a purpose into the tough will of her.

As they turned into the yard of the courthouse they saw Joe Kneen unlocking the door. When they walked in he had hung his hat on its nail and was looking at his desk, on which he had placed his mail. They surprised a look of worry, almost disillusion on his face as he looked at the pile of letters.

Hearing them, he glanced up, and immediately the caution came back into his eyes. He greeted them tiredly and pushed a chair toward Celia, and she sat down.

She looked at Will and nodded for him to talk, and Will said, "We know what happened to John," and told him. He spared none of the details of what had passed at Ten Mile, and as he moved deeper into the account of the girl at Red Courteen's he saw a sadness creep into Kneen's face.

When he finished Kneen walked to the door and stood in it, back to them, his shoulder bowed, his hands rammed deep into his hip pockets. Turning presently, he said in a tired voice, "All right, Will. I'll do what I can."

Celia said, "Do you believe, like Will and I, Cavanaugh did kill him?"

Kneen only nodded and looked with bleak curiosity at Will. He saw the marks of a fight on the big man, and a kind of bitter discouragement was in his voice as he said,

"You've been out to his place?"

Will nodded assent and said quietly, "If I get to him first, Joe, I'm not going to wait for you."

"Then you'll be tried too," Kneen said somberly.

Will only nodded and looked at Celia, and she rose.

Kneen said in a discouraged voice, "That's a fool's gamble, Will. Let him come to trial."

Will was silent a moment and then said dryly, "Suppose I do, Joe. Tell me what will happen." Kneen didn't answer, and Will went on: "This whole country's set to tear Hatchet apart. Try to get a jury that doesn't hate us. Try to get a jury that will try Cavanaugh and not Hatchet. Can you promise to get one, Joe?"

Kneen shook his head, and his voice was tired and sad. "No, I can't promise that, Will."

"That's why I won't wait for you, Joe," Will murmured.

Celia came over to Kneen then. "It's not easy for you, is it, Mr. Kneen?" she said in a low voice.

Kneen grimaced and shook his head and

said, "No. Thank you for seeing it," and he was again staring bitterly at the stack of mail on his desk when they stepped out.

Chapter 10

Marriner rode into town at dusk and went straight to the courthouse and found Kneen was not in. He sent the three men with him on ahead and walked down to the Belle Fourche and was told there by the bartender that Kneen and a dozen men were off looking for Cavanaugh. Cavanaugh had killed John Evarts, the bartender said.

Bide listened impatiently, and without commenting he went over to a poker game and took a chair. He played erratically and impatiently and won, as he usually did, but the game lacked flavor tonight. He constantly watched the door and every hour or so asked for word of Kneen, and when the game broke up he stayed on playing a game of blackjack with the houseman.

The stage from the reservation pulled in at midnight, and the driver came in for a drink, and Marriner gossiped with him a few minutes at the bar. But he was too restless for talk and he went out into the night. There were lamps still lighted in the hotel, and he went over to it and wakened the clerk, who sleepily sold him a dozen of his favorite cigars and went back to bed.

Marriner fired up a smoke out on the sidewalk and paced down a block, crossed the street, came back, and poked his head in the Belle Fourche. Kneen wasn't in yet, they said inside.

Marriner threw his cigar away and swore in disgust. Kneen, he supposed, would be gone for a day or so. Reluctantly he went back to the courthouse and picked up his horse and rode it back to the main street, turning south and heading for home.

But he looked back once, just to be sure, and was surprised to see several horses at the Belle Fourche's tie rail. He turned back, and when he was close enough to identify the horses he gave a grunt of satisfaction. Kneen's horse was among them.

Inside the Belle Fourche a half-dozen possemen, along with Kneen, were drinking at the bar in silent weariness.

Marrier caught Kneen's eye in the back-bar mirror and motioned with his head toward the rear of the saloon and walked toward the back room. Kneen finished his drink and said to the men, "Tomorrow at seven," and followed Marriner into one of the back rooms.

Bide was standing by a poker table, his head and shoulders out of the light from the overhead lamp, when Kneen came in and closed the door behind him and said, "What is it, Bide?"

"Cavanaugh's at my place."

Kneen stood motionless while he digested this, trying to see Bide's face in the shadow and failing.

He shoved a chair toward Marriner and took one himself, sighing as he sat down. Marriner pulled the chair around and put his foot on it and crossed his arms, resting them on his knee. When his face came into the light of the lamp Kneen was shocked at the excitement and pleasure in it.

Kneen put an arm on the table and said dryly, "It's queer he came to you."

Marriner grinned. He had a raffish smile that annoyed Kneen as much as his mocking black eyes.

"Don't start thinkin' things, Joe," Marriner said in complete good humor.

"Just listen. I want him arrested and tried."

Kneen said impatiently, "Wait. Start from the beginning."

"That's all there is. Cavanaugh said the day after Will set us afoot out there he was at Kennedy's place. He'd made it that far, wet as hell and tired. Next mornin' it was still rainin', and he was comin' down sick. There at Kennedy's."

Kneen listened carefully, a distaste for this already within him. Marriner went on, "Evarts come up in the rain and asked for him, and when he come out Evarts told him to get off the place."

"Kennedy's place?" Kneen asked sharply.

Marriner nodded. "Ray told him to go to hell. Evarts pulled a gun on him, and Ray ran back into the shack. Evarts came in shootin'—all misses. Ray found his gun, and when he came up with it Evarts ran. Ray shot him."

Marriner ceased talking, his bright eyes watching every expression in Kneen's face.

"In the back," Kneen said dryly.

"That's right. Ray and Wes Kennedy buried Evarts up in the timber above Kennedy's place. They knew damn well Ballard wouldn't believe Ray shot in self-defense. Well, Kennedy lost his nerve and lit out. Ray knew he would talk, so he came to me."

Kneen's lip curled in contempt. He said bitterly, "Do you believe that yarn, Bide?"

"Hell, no."

Kneen was puzzled now. He studied Marriner's swarthy, mocking face which held a subdued and malicious pleasure, and he tried to explain it and could not. He said, "You want me to arrest Ray and hold him for trial?"

"That's what you do with a man who admits he killed someone, don't you?"

Kneen said sharply, "What do you want out of this, Bide?"

"Justice—simple justice," Bide said, laughing.

For a moment Kneen just stared, and then it came to him—the conversation with Will Ballard this morning and Will's quietly cynical prediction of what would happen when Ray Cavanaugh was put on trial. Bide Marriner was shrewd enough to see this too.

Kneen used Will's words. "You mean you want Hatchet tried."

"That's just what I mean," Marriner said flatly. He wasn't smiling now, and his voice lost its mockery as he spoke. "Put Cavanaugh on trial and we've broken Hatchet. No jury in this country would hang a man that Hatchet wanted hung. And when Ballard sees that he'll give up. He can't fight. He'll clear out—even a stubborn wild man like Will Ballard."

Kneen said coldly, "That's one way to lick Hatchet all right."

"And legal," Bide said, and he laughed.

Kneen stood up. "It's a way I won't have anything to do with, Bide."

Bide's smile faded and he said gently, "Joe, you can't do anythin' about it. The law says you've got to. You're like a train on a track from now on. You go straight to the end of the line. The law says so."

He unfolded his arms and came erect and watched Kneen with a burning malice in his eyes. He had Kneen where we wanted him, and he didn't bother to hide his satisfaction.

Kneen's fisted hand on the table was white. He said with a harsh pleading in his voice, "But John Evarts was shot in the back! Don't that mean anything to you?"

"Nothin'," Bide said flatly. "I didn't kill him, Cavanaugh did. And Cavanaugh will go on trial for it. If that's to my advantage no man can say I'm to blame."

He turned to the door and put a hand on the knob and said, "When do you want him, Joe?"

Kneen stared at him for a long moment, and Bide met his glance unswervingly.

Kneen said bleakly then, "I'll be out."

"Don't wait too long, Joe," Bide taunted. "The word will be out tomorrow. You got your job to do."

He closed the door softly behind him, and Kneen stood quietly in front of his chair. He was thinking, *Like a train. You go straight to the end of the track. The law says so.* He reached up and turned down the lamp and walked slowly toward the door. His hand on the knob, he paused. Behind the dozen things that were pushing at him he saw only one thing clearly: Ray Cavanaugh, an admitted killer, would go free. He suddenly hated Bide Marriner with a bitter, scalding vehemence.

Chapter 11

In midmorning Red Courteen rode into Boundary with his crew and left them at the Belle Fourche. He went first to the barbershop, and while his hair was being cut he learned of Ray Cavanaugh's confession to the shooting of John Evarts. Talk of it obscurely annoyed Red, and the barber, sensing this, was silent while he shaved him.

Red lay with his eyes closed, the hot towel on his face, and wondered how this news would affect his own plans. If they were plans, that is. Red couldn't make up his mind about it. He'd left Ten Mile on impulse, aided by a few drinks under his belt. Now this morning he wasn't so sure.

He paid the barber and stepped out into the street and glanced over at the Belle Fourche. He would have liked to go over and yarn with the boys over a few drinks, but this thing kept nagging at him. *Then get it over with*, he thought. *The worst he can say is no.*

With sudden decision he turned upstreet, and already he felt better. He passed the hotel and the four corners, his pace leisurely and holding a faint truculence, and kept on upstreet and presently he turned into Priest's Emporium and sauntered down the aisle. The store was busy, and he spotted Priest over at the grocery counter, waiting on a woman. Red waited quietly, watching Priest, really looking at him for the first time, because he might do business with him. Red noted the cold, polite manner of the man, the skill with which he chatted with the woman about her family and her affairs and remained underneath totally disinterested. A hard man, Red thought with dislike, but maybe that would help.

When the woman said good-by Red stepped over to the counter and said, "How are you, Mr. Priest?"

"You're off your reservation, aren't you, Courteen?" Priest said, his effortless smile of greeting very thin because of Red's reputation.

Red nodded and said idly, watching Priest, "Talked with Garretson the other night. Thought I'd drop over."

Priest's eyes were wary, unresponsive. "How is Harve?"

"Maybe," Red suggested, looking around him, "there's someplace we can talk."

Priest hesitated a moment, and then his curiosity conquered, as Red knew it would. Priest came out from behind the counter and led him to the back of the store, out onto the loading platform, and then into the warehouse. It was quiet and private in here and it smelled of the cold iron of stored stoves.

Red put a foot on a keg of nails and reached for his tobacco in his shirt pocket.

"Please don't smoke in here," Priest said quietly. "There's powder in here."

Red's hand fell away, and he looked obliquely at Priest before he sat down on the keg of nails. His tough-shaped face held a puzzlement and a mild embarrassment; he wasn't used to dealing with men like Priest. The storekeeper stood ramrod straight, watching him with a faint distaste in his face.

Courteen said mildly, "That's a hard thing Ballard did to Garretson over those cattle."

"Yes," Priest said.

"Your cattle, too, weren't they?"

Priest hesitated, and Red said in a friendly voice, "Hell, I'm just tellin' you what Garretson told me. He was on the prod the other night."

Still Priest didn't say anything, and Red decided to get down to business. "How you goin' get 'em back, Priest? Does Ballard aim to treat you different on account of Lottie?"

Priest said firmly, "That's no business of yours."

"You mean he won't make an exception." Red smiled faintly and murmured, "Not Will Ballard, if I know him." He looked sharply at Priest now. "He can't hold 'em under the law. You know that."

Priest relented a little and nodded.

"How bad you want 'em back?" Red drawled.

Priest studied him a moment and then murmured dryly, "Personally, I never take an order unless I can deliver the goods. It's a good rule to follow."

Red smiled; he was understood. "I can deliver."

"How?"

"Take 'em away from him."

Priest looked skeptical, but he said, "And

what's your share for doing the job?"

Red laughed now. "Not one damn penny, friend."

Priest scowled. He put his thin hands on his hips and spread his legs a little and studied Courteen closely and finally said, "That's hard for me to understand."

"Not if you saw what happened in Ten Mile the other night." A faint angry flush came to his face as he thought of it, and he said grimly, "Will Ballard wrecked my place. Just for the hell of it."

"And you'd like to return the call?"

"I'd like to have an excuse to," Red corrected softly. He rose and spoke to Priest in a low, earnest voice. "Look, Priest. I can't ride into Hatchet and brace Ballard. You know that. Kneen doesn't like anythin' about me and Ten Mile, and that's the excuse he'd need to close me out. But if I go to Hatchet and demand my own cattle that Ballard's holdin' illegally and he tries to stop me I'm within my rights."

"Your cattle?" Priest said suspiciously.

"Make me out a bill of sale for those cattle," Red said impatiently. "Date it yesterday. I'll write you out one and date it today, and you can hold it. I tell you, I don't want anythin' out of this except an excuse to get into Hatchet."

Priest said slowly, "What if there's trouble?"

"Why do you think I've got my crew outside?" Red murmured. "Well, what about it?"

Priest clasped his hands behind him under his coattails and walked to the door. There was a set of scales by the door, and some ingrained love of order prompted Priest to shove the scale weight along the sliding bar until it reached zero. Then he stood there, nervously slapping the back of one hand in the palm of the other behind him.

He turned suddenly and came back and said, "What does Garretson say?"

"Whatever you say."

Red watched him, knowing exactly what was in Priest's mind. His love of a dollar was battling with his reluctance to do business with a man suspected of whisky peddling and cattle stealing. But the thing that weighted the scales in his favor, Red knew, was that Priest believed himself within his rights. Ballard couldn't hold those cattle, according to law.

Priest made a wry face and shook his

head. "I don't like this."

Red said dryly, "I'm a black sheep, maybe, but the color don't rub off, Priest."

Priest flushed. He hesitated a moment longer and then said curtly, "Come along. We'll sign the bills of sale," and started for the door.

A profound pleasure was on Red's tough face as he followed him.

Joe Kneen slept late this morning. He lived alone in a single room at the Stockman's House, and waking up this morning had not been a pleasure. As he dressed he would pause now and then and stare at the drab paper on the wall, his thoughts raveling off at some remembered phrase of Bide's last night.

He went on into the hotel dining room. It was empty, and he took a table at a window that looked out onto the side street.

His breakfast, always the same, was brought him. He pushed the steak and potatoes around on the plate a few times and then shoved the plate away from him. He was not hungry and, from the way he felt, he didn't think he'd ever be hungry again. He drank his coffee, mulling over his conversation with Bide last night. The irony of his position was, in the last analysis, what discouraged him. He had believed a month ago with all his heart that Hatchet was breaking up and its dissolution should be hurried. For Joe Kneen had been one of the fifteen men who hit Boundary the day Phil Evarts did, and that night they had slept next to each other on the floor of the trading post for the Indians, the lone building in this country.

Joe remembered the first month here, how Phil Evarts left the saddle just long enough to rock up the monuments that were to mark his homestead. The rest of the time Phil rode, camping with other newcomers, listening to their talk, sharing their food, and all the time he was observing and scheming. He didn't come back to his homestead until he had chosen the range and set the boundaries of Hatchet, and it didn't matter at all to him in his fabulous arrogance that these boundaries blanketed the claims of dozens of other settlers. Phil was that way, and all the years Joe had known him he had ridden roughshod over other men, fighting, bribing, threatening, and taking, until everything between those original boundaries was his.

So Joe saw no wrong in breaking up Hatchet after Phil's death, saw no shame in siding in with Bide Marriner, who would do the breaking.

But now where was he? He wiped his mustache and rose and went outside, pausing at the desk to buy a cigar. Stepping down from the porch to the plank walk, it came to him that he must make up his mind about this today. Now. Either he must be honest enough to admit that Will Ballard's steadfast opinion that Bide Marriner was a greedier man than Phil had ever been was right, or he must side in with Bide. Joe Kneen, in his cautious way, held little brief for Will Ballard's wild ways, but they were preferable to Bide's. If he threw in with Will he could at least look a man squarely in the eyes, and that was his choice.

He crossed the street and nodded to the men lounging around the front of the Belle Fourche. There ahead of Kneen, his shoulder laid against the corner of the saloon, was a man he couldn't place instantly. And then it came to him that this was one of Will Ballard's new hands; he had ridden in the posse with them yesterday. His name, Joe remembered now, was Young, and when he came up to him Young nodded civilly and drawled, "You ready to ride, Mister Kneen?" Joe removed the cigar from his mouth and asked quietly, "Heard about Cavanaugh?"

Jim Young grinned disarmingly. "That's what I was tryin' to ask you."

Joe knew a hard moment of doubt, and then he plunged headlong. It was the hardest decision he had ever made, and he didn't know he had made it until after he spoke.

"I'm going out to get him at Bib M today," he said softly. "I'll bring him back alone late tonight. Can you tell Will that?"

Jim Young looked steadily at him, his eyes at once cautious and alert and skeptical. He didn't answer for a long moment, turning this over in his mind, and when he was sure it added up to what he thought it did he said, "I'll tell him."

"Be sure and tell him," Kneen said wearily, and he went on.

Jim Young watched Kneen's back for a long minute, still wondering if he had heard rightly. Then the overwhelming importance of getting this word to Will occurred to him, and he moved toward his horse.

He paused to let a man pass in front of

him and heard a familiar voice say, "Where you been, kid?"

He looked up and saw Red Courteen standing there, grinning.

"Around some," Jim Young said carefully. He hadn't seen Courteen since the night in Ten Mile when he and Mel were persuaded to move onto Hatchet.

"You and your brother have any trouble gettin' range?" Red asked.

Jim smiled. "Easiest thing I ever done," he murmured. He dodged under the hitch rail and untied his horse, and Courteen, mildly curious, put his hands on the rail and said, "What happened with Ballard?"

Jim stepped into the saddle and said gravely, "I pulled his arm off and beat him over the head with it until he made me a partner."

He pulled his horse around sideways to Courteen and pointed solemnly at the Hatchet brand on the horse's left hip. Courteen's angry glance fell on it, and he stared.

Jim Young winked gravely and moved out into the traffic of the street, and already he was casting about for the place to find Will Ballard.

Chapter 12

For the second time within a week Will rode the trails under Indian Ridge, and this time he did not care if he was seen. He rode boldly into the small hill ranches where men answered him sullenly until they learned his business. Then they invited him to see for himself, for none of them wanted to be accused of hiding the man who murdered John Evarts. Will spread the word and gave the warning, and the fact that he rode alone with the marks of his fight still on him impressed them. Hatchet finally was on the warpath, and they did not have Bide Marriner to stiffen their backs.

When Will finished the circuit he dropped back to Cavanaugh's place. There was a small chance that Cavanaugh still did not know Will was hunting him and had returned to his shack. Will didn't believe this, but it was a way of shoring up his patience. Sooner or later, if he was patient enough, somebody's careless word or glance, a track, a warm campfire would put him on Cavanaugh's trail. Until then he must wait and watch.

He dropped down into the valley where Cavanaugh's shack lay sometime during the night and came up on it as he had done before. This time, too, when he struck his match inside the shack he found it empty. He looked about him, noting the wreckage was not as he had left it. The table was propped upright against the wall, and the lamp was on it. He went over and lighted the lamp and saw the blood smeared on its base, and he knew Sam had placed it there. The wrecked bunk had been leveled out on the dirt floor, and its blankets were straightened out. Will took the lamp and stood over the bunk, and he saw the blood and the soot smears at the head of the blankets. He knew Sam had dragged himself to it and slept off his beating. He wondered idly about Sam, knowing his pride was as stubborn as his anger. He judged Sam would sulk for a time before he faced Celia and Hatchet again.

Will waited out the night in these

blankets, and by daylight he was in the saddle again, headed for Kennedy's place.

It was here that Jim Young found him in midafternoon. To explain Kneen's message, Jim Young first had to tell him of the story current in Boundary—of how Cavanaugh had been forced in self-protection to shoot John, so had shot him in the back and fled to Bide to give himself up. The bald arrogance of the lie was still in Will's mind when Young gave him Kneen's message. They were sitting on the porch, and Jim watched Will's face as he told him.

There was unbelief in it, and Will asked him to repeat the message, and he did. When he was finished Will stared off at the distant timber for several minutes, and when he returned his gaze to Jim there was a strange somberness in his eyes. "How did Kneen look?"

"Tired, I reckon. Fed up. Mad. I couldn't rightly tell."

Will thought he knew, now. Kneen had gagged at the job ahead of him. When Will and Celia had talked to him he had shown plainly that he knew what might happen if Cavanaugh was caught and did not like it. Faced with it at last, Kneen had revolted, and Will knew that he had gravely misjudged Kneen and was sorry for it. And now Will knew what he must do and he did not like it either, knowing, nevertheless, he was going through with it.

He walked over to his horse and said, "You go back to Hatchet, Jim."

"Sure you don't want me to side you?" Jim Young asked.

Will shook his head in negation and rode out.

He traveled steadily through the waning afternoon and dusk and into the early evening, and a short time after complete dark he came to the spot he had decided upon.

It was where the road from Bib M to town skirted a thick stand of pine timber. Across the road the land sloped gently down onto bare flats. The timber afforded a hiding place, while any rider passing him would be silhouetted against the open grassland that was gray in the dark night.

He sat beside his horse back in the timber, listening to the night sounds, his ears straining to catch the sound of approaching riders. He tried to think of other things, but his mind came back always to what was before him, and his thoughts were gray and bleak.

It was sometime around midnight when he picked up the sound of horses coming down the road from Bib M. He stepped into the saddle and moved over the deep, soft humus of pine needles to the edge of the timber above the road. His horse snorted softly, and he did not reprimand him.

And then the indistinct bulk of two riders slowly took shape on the road below him, and he put his horse down to the road too. The pair of horsemen stopped, and Will approached them slowly and said, "Joe?"

He heard Cavanaugh's quick, excited voice. "That's Will Ballard!"

Will reined up and said, "Give him your gun, Joe."

There was a thud as something landed in the road, and Kneen's weary voice said, "I threw it in the road." To Cavanaugh he said, "Pick it up, Ray," and pulled his horse off the road.

For perhaps ten seconds there was utter silence, and then Cavanaugh yelled: "Joe! Joe! You can't do this! I've surrendered! Joe!"

He ceased talking, and Will said gently,

"Pick it up, Ray. Only hurry."

Cavanaugh's shrill voice again lifted into the night. "No! No! I won't take it. I've surrendered!" He pulled his horse over toward Kneen until Will saw their two horses merge into one dark bulk.

He heard a grunt and immediately afterward the solid thud of flesh on flesh and he heard Cavanaugh's cry, and then the shape of the dark mass was altered. Part of it was in the road now. It was Cavanaugh; Kneen had knocked him from the saddle.

Kneen said with a cold, wintry fury in his voice, "You'll take that gun if I have to strap it in your hand!" And again he moved away from Cavanaugh's horse.

Will saw Cavanaugh come to his feet, heard his terrified sob, and then he saw him lunge for the gun in the road.

Will waited, motionless, peering at the dark, sobbing shape in the road ahead of him. He saw Cavanaugh rise and run for his horse, and then the flash and the shot came.

Will waited another moment until he heard Cavanaugh hit the saddle, and then he roweled his horse and reached for his own gun.

Cavanaugh shot again and pulled his

horse around and put it down the slope onto the grass, and Will, implacable, cut across the road, too, and was after him.

The race was wordless, desperate, and the urgency of it seemed communicated to the horses. The shape of Cavanaugh's horse ahead of him was distinct against the grass. Will pulled his horse to the left a bit, trying to head Cavanaugh off from the island of timber that bulked darkly to the south. But Cavanaugh had seen it and was heading for it.

Again Cavanaugh shot and again missed, and Will saw that his own horse was overhauling Cavanaugh's. He was twenty feet behind him now, and he raised his gun.

Cavanaugh, as if sensing Will's intention, shot again, and Will lowered his gun. Cavanaugh's dark shape ahead of him was too cunningly blended with the trees.

They hit the timber in a headlong gallop, Cavanaugh in the lead. He plunged his horse recklessly into it, and Will, hugging the neck of his horse, followed. He heard the breaking of brush ahead, heard the frightened snort of Cavanaugh's horse, and then came a sharp crack of a breaking limb and the smothered cry on the heel of it, and then the sound of Cavanaugh hitting the underbrush.

Will reined up violently, and the sound of crashing brush ahead of him he roweled his horse toward it.

The shot came then, and it was almost at the head of his horse, a blinding flash.

Will kneed his horse on with a savage violence, and he felt his horse hit Cavanaugh and he held his gun down and shot. It took his horse ten feet to check its run, and Will reined up and listened. Off somewhere to the left Cavanaugh's horse was moving around.

Will rode back and dismounted, and now he could make out Cavanaugh's lighter shirt in the brush. He waited a moment, listening, and then reached for a match and wiped it alight with his fingernail.

He saw Cavanaugh then and put his match out immediatley and turned away, fighting a sickness. His long shot had caught Cavanaugh in the face.

He mounted then and rode slowly back to the road. Kneen was sitting by the side of it, smoking. He threw away his cigarette and stood up as Will's horse climbed the shoulder of the road and halted beside him.

"He's back there in the timber," Will said. "I made a mistake about you, Joe, and I'm sorry for it."

"All right."

Will's voice was troubled now. "They won't go easy on you, Joe."

"Not on either of us," Kneen said meagerly.

Will was silent a moment, and then he asked, "Did he tell you where he buried John?"

"On the north slope above the shack."

Neither of them spoke for a moment, and then Kneen sighed softly. "I feel better, Will. What kind of a man am I for saying that?"

"An honest one."

"I think I am," Kneen said quietly, and he mounted and put his horse down the slope.

Chapter 13

Red Courteen said, "When this starts, Mitch, you circle behind the bunkhouse and watch from the upside."

He saw the two men standing in the door of Hatchet's bunkhouse in the late-afternoon sun. One was Ike Adams and the other, Red saw, was the brother of the fresh Texas kid he'd seen in town this morning, but he rode on, unimpressed.

His eight men spread out a little behind him, and Mitch dropped out to drift behind the bunkhouse. Red reined up in front of the bunkhouse steps where Ike stood.

"What do you want here, Red?" Ike asked sourly. He held a carbine slacked in his arm.

Red didn't answer immediately. The Texan was behind Ike. In the cookshack doorway, Red noted, the cook stood with a six-gun tucked in the top of his apron.

Red's glance settled now on Ike and he said, "Cattle."

"If we got any of yours in there it's a mistake."

Red smiled faintly. "You got a hundred of mine, Ike, and it's not mistake." He reached in his shirt pocket for Priest's bill of sale and gave it to Ike, glancing lazily, indifferently, at the house as he did so. He was still looking at it as Ike unfolded the bill of sale and read it.

Only when he heard the paper tear did he look down at Ike. Carefully, disdainfully, Ike was tearing the bill of sale in quarters, eights, and finally sixteenths. Then he threw the pieces on the ground and said, "They stay in the pasture, Red."

Red said unsmilingly, "All right, boys."

Ike's carbine came up, cocked. "Just ride back the way you come. I'll follow you a ways."

Red murmured dryly, "Eight to three, Ike. Pick out your man, because you won't get a second shot."

Ike's gun swung over to cover him. "I'll take you then," Ike said quietly.

For a moment nobody moved. Red waited patiently, watching Ike, gauging his intention. He knew Ike would shoot; he also figured that Mitch had had plenty of time to skirt the bunkhouse, cover Ike, and put a stop to this. He said then, "Ike, you're covered. Figure it out. Now put that gun down and shut up."

Ike's rifle mounted to his shoulder, and for one wild instant of unbelief Red saw that he really intended to shoot. He rolled out of the saddle just as Mitch's gun blasted from the upper corner of the bunkhouse. Ike shot, too, but it was only reflex as he was driven to his knees by Mitch's bullet.

The whole thing exploded then, and Red saw it with a kind of horror, knowing it was too late to stop it. The Texan dodged back in the bunkhouse and slammed the door. The cook did the same in the cookshack. Half his men were shooting now at the door of the bunkhouse while they scattered for cover.

Red himself ran to the upper corner of the bunkhouse and came in beside Mitch.

"He was goin' to shoot you!" Mitch said excitedly.

Red said savagely, "Ah, you damn fool!" and peered around the corner. His men had taken to cover at the corral and the barn.

The Texan now calmly walked out from the bunkhouse, picked Ike up, and went inside with him. Red cursed bitterly. This was all wrong, but it had gone too far now for him to back out. He might as well go through with it as planned. He went to the other corner of the bunkhouse and shouted orders for three of his men to drive all the cattle out of the pasture. He detailed two more to keep the cook and the Texan inside the bunkhouse and ordered the rest to make their way to the house. As he was calling he felt Mitch's hand on his arm and he shook it off impatiently. When he was finished, however, Mitch said, "Look," and pointed to the house.

Red turned to see Celia Evarts, skirts lifted in both hands, running toward the bunkhouse.

Red waited in doubt only a moment, and then he ran out to intercept her. Celia saw him coming and tried to dodge, and Red caught her. Picking her up, arm around her waist, he started back to the house with her. Celia fought furiously, but Red covered his face with his free arm and went on. When he reached the porch he set her down just as two of his men who had ridden in a wide circle out of range of the cook's six-gun arrived at the house.

Celia looked at them wrathfully and said, "Ike's shot! I want to see him."

Red said grimly, "Afterward. You're goin' to stay right here now," and turned to two of his men. "Bring her along."

Red strode past her and into the doorway of the living room. Celia, still struggling, was escorted into the living room by two of Red's men, who almost carried her between them.

But when Celia was inside she stopped struggling and only watched Red Courteen. With his gun Red smashed everything breakable that he could see in the room. He overturned chairs, kicking their backs out, put a boot through the back of the sofa, and threw the table through the window. Celia watched first with astonishment and then with furious contempt in her face, while outside the shooting kept up with a maddening regularity. Room by room Celia was forced to watch Red smash everything he could reach. He worked with the vicious concentration of a destructive child, and Celia was almost afraid of what she saw in his tough face. She didn't know why he was doing it, could not understand the almost fanatical pleasure he was getting out of this destruction. He saved her bedroom until the last, and when that was thoroughly wrecked he went back out onto the veranda.

He stood there, eyes alight with a wicked pleasure, breathing deeply from his exertion. Even his men, Celia noticed, were a little sobered by what they had seen. She kept silent, hoping they would go so she could see Ike. Mel Young in the bunkhouse and the cook in the cookshack were still futilely shooting.

Red glanced down toward the corrals and saw the cattle streaming out of the pasture, and then he turned to Celia.

"Give Will Ballard a look at that," he said flatly, nodding toward the house. "Next time he wrecks Ten Mile for me he'll think twice."

"He'll finish it next time," Celia said scornfully. "I think, Mr. Courteen, you'll leave the country if you're wise."

Red smiled thinly. "You can tell Will why Ike was shot too. I had a bill of sale for a hundred cattle I'd bought from Priest. Ike wouldn't honor it. Tell him that."

Celia didn't answer, and her silence

seemed to enrage Courteen. He said thickly, "I took a lot off your old man and Will Ballard when Hatchet was top of the heap. I aim to show you and Ballard how it feels."

He turned and mounted his horse, and his two men followed him down to the corral. On the way he pulled off the two men who had kept Mel Young and the cook in the bunkhouse.

Celia hurried to the bunkhouse through the dusk now, and Mel Young opened the door for her. She went straight to Ike's bunk and knelt beside him. He was propped up on his elbows, his truculent face pale and twisted with pain, and he said angrily, "Mel said they cornered you up in the house."

"It doesn't matter, Ike," Celia said hastily. "Where are you hit?"

"The leg," Ike said weakly.

She looked at the wound, which was a clean shot through the thick part of the thigh. While Mel Young lighted the lamp against the deepening dusk and then went for hot water with the cook, Celia set about dressing Ike's leg.

Neither of them talked, and Celia worked with a feverish concentration, trying to crowd out of her mind any memory of what had happened. But try as she might, she could not forget one thing Red Courteen had told her. Ike was shot because he refused to honor Courteen's bill of sale from Lowell Priest. Celia, thinking of that and of Lottie, thought then of Will and pitied him.

Sam was roused by a racketing knock at his door, and he shouted sleepily, "Who is it?"

Before the answer came he noted irritably that it was daylight, and then someone shouted, "Russ Schultz, Sam."

"Come in," Sam said sullenly.

He swung out of bed, wincing against the soreness of his body, pulled on his pants, and then looked over at Schultz in the doorway.

Schultz was excited, but in spite of it he paused, staring at Sam's face. It was swollen and cut, both eyes purple and scarcely open. Sam flushed under his glance and said angrily through swollen lips, "What do you want?"

Schultz said, "Will got him."

Sam came slowly off the bed, and Schultz began to tell of what happened. Kneen had left late last evening with Cavanaugh to take him to jail. He'd returned to Bib M after midnight with Cavanaugh's body. Kneen's story was that Cavanaugh had tried to escape and he'd shot him. Bide had doubted immediately that Cavanaugh even wanted to escape, and when he'd looked at Cavanaugh and seen where he was shot he was sure. At the crack of daylight this morning Bide had taken his crew and Kneen out to the scene of the shooting. Sure enough, there were the tracks of a third horse, which could only be Will Ballard's.

Sam listened carefully, his own troubles forgotten. His thick chest was bruised and red, but he made no effort to hide the marks as he became absorbed in Schultz's story.

Schultz finished, "So Bide wants you as a witness. He's waitin' down there with Kneen for you."

Sam said, "Of course," and picked up his shirt. He was so excited that he buttoned his shirt crookedly, did not think of breakfast, and did not bother after he was dressed to tidy his room, a chore he had not once neglected since he'd built this place. He felt only a growing elation; Will had gone too far at long last.

He stepped out into a gray morning. The

smell of pine pitch and chips was strong in the air as he passed his new bunkhouse of peeled logs and saw that his crew had already scattered for the day's work.

Catching up his horse quickly, he saddled him and met Schultz in front of the house, and they rode out.

They came on Bide and his crew a half-hour later. Bide, with Kneen, was seated on the shoulder of the wagon road where it rounded the curve of a timbered slope. The horses of Bide's crew were all being held together down off the slope, the men with them.

Bide rose as Sam approached and called, "Pull off the road on the upside, Sam."

Sam did so and came up to them and dismounted. He was grateful that nobody seemed to notice his bruised face. Kneen didn't rise, only nodded in quiet greeting. Bide's dark face held less anger than impatience, and he said grimly, "I didn't want you to spoil the tracks. Did Schultz tell you?"

Sam nodded, and Bide beckoned him down to the road. Once there, Bide reconstructed what had happened. He talked crisply, a curious impatience edging his voice, and not once did he look at Kneen or try to hide anything from Kneen's hearing. He was talking with a purpose, his confidence hard and undoubting.

Finished on the road, he guided Sam down the slope, and they rode over to the small island of timber a quarter of a mile away.

Here again Bide patiently reconstructed what had happened, finally showing him the brush where Cavanaugh had fallen. A fleeting, unwanted thought passed through Sam's mind as he listened. Even the cold and factual reconstruction somehow made Will Ballard seem as implacable as death.

When Bide was finished they walked to the edge of the timber, and Bide pulled out tobacco from his old Mackinaw pocket. Nervously he rolled a thin cigarette and lighted it and then turned to Sam. For the first time now Sam was aware that Bide was looking at his bruised face with open curiosity. Sam also rolled a cigarette, offering no information.

Bide said crisply then, "Sam, we've been pretty fair neighbors, haven't we? At least you strike me as a reasonable man."

Sam grunted assent.

"I called you this mornin' for two reasons. I wanted a witness to what I'd found, somebody besides my own crew. There was another reason."

Sam glanced obliquely at him.

"I'm out to get Will Ballard, and if I have to wreck Hatchet to do it, I will." Only as he spoke now did he betray the full measure of his anger. It was bitter, depthless, obsessing him.

Sam felt a hot pleasure at seeing it, and he asked meagerly, "Where do you think I picked up these marks?"

"Will?" When Sam nodded Bide said, "All right. Are you with me?"

"I hope I'm ahead of you," Sam said quietly.

They rode back to Kneen now, and Sam pulled up beside him. "Is that what happened, Joe?"

Kneen looked at him almost dully and murmured tonelessly, "Ray tried to escape and I shot him."

Marriner rode up then and said, "Go back to town, Joe. We're through with you."

His voice was contemptuous, and a bright anger flared in Kneen's pale eyes. "Don't be too sure of that, Bide."

Bide didn't smile, didn't even let on he'd heard him. One of the men led a pack horse down out of the timber, and Sam saw the canvas-wrapped burden on its back. Kneen mounted, took the lead rope of the pack horse, and set off to town.

Sam was suddenly aware that Bide was eyeing him challengingly. "I'm takin' my men to Hatchet to wait for Will. You comin'?"

Sam nodded, no longer afraid of having to face Celia.

Chapter 14

Ike dropped into a deep sleep in the middle of the morning, and Celia, for the first time since the afternoon before, felt at a loss. She and the Youngs had taken turns nursing Ike through a feverish night, and now she felt tired and somehow useless.

She wandered through the rooms of the house that Red had wrecked yesterday, and they had for her now a nightmare quality about them. She looked at the wreck of the massive old dresser with its shattered glass and tried to feel angry at its destruction. Her father had bribed an Indian freighter to haul it from the East to the agency along with his trade goods. That was long before the railroad was here, and her father and his men had freighted it themselves the last leg of the journey over the Indigos to Hatchet. Her mother had valued it above all her other possessions, and now it lay on its face, the glass shattered, its back kicked in—and Celia felt nothing. Things had come too fast this past week and dwarfed all this in importance. There was nobody to turn to, either, for Sam had not shown his face, and Will had not slept here in ten nights. In that time John Evarts had been killed, and she had come into Hatchet. Her world had changed entirely, except for Will. Yet he had changed, too, slipping into that part of a man's world where a woman could not follow. It frightened Celia when she thought of how it had come about. She knew now that Will had expected it all along and that she hadn't, really. She had agreed with Will and listened to him, but it was words they were dealing with, not happenings. Not any more, though. He had fought with Sam and was riding the hills, hunting a man, and she looked out at the gray day and shivered. She suddenly wanted to see Will and talk to him more than anything in the world, and for a moment she pitied herself and hated herself for it immediately.

She went out to the bunkhouse then and got Jim Young and brought him back to the house, and together they set about clearing up the wreckage. She worked furiously, wordlessly, leaving the heaviest jobs for him, but trying to exhaust herself with work.

She had swept up a great pile of broken glass in the office when she heard Jim Young's steps in the corridor and looked up.

He came in and said cautiously, "A bunch of riders are comin' in, Miss Evarts. Mr. Danfelser's with 'em, though. That's all right, isn't it?"

"It's all right, Jim."

Celia left her work and went back through the corridor out onto the porch. Ten or so men were dismounting under the cottonwoods, among them Sam. And then she saw Bide Marriner, and a quick fear came to her.

Sam came up to her first, and she knew by the arrogance in his heavy stride that he had not forgiven her. She had seen the way Will was marked by the fight at Cavanaugh's, but Sam's face shocked her. She sensed immediately that he had made a great concession to his stubborn pride in coming here to face her, and she was sorry for him. Now looking beyond him, she saw Bide start for the porch, too, and she said quickly, distrustfully, "Why are you riding with him, Sam?"

Sam didn't answer but waited until Bide

came up. Marriner touched his hat, and Celia nodded coldly.

Marriner spoke first. "This isn't Sam's job, Miss Evarts, so I might as well tell you why we've come." He hesitated and said dryly, "Have you heard that Will Ballard shot Cavanaugh last night?"

Sam said in an outraged voice, "Kneen let him."

"I'm glad," Celia said quietly.

Marriner looked almost shocked. "That's an odd sentiment to come from a lady."

"Not when you stop to think about it, Bide," Celia said levelly. "What do you want?"

"We're going to wait here for Will."

Celia looked instantly at Sam. "Are they, Sam?"

Sam's face flushed, and he said angrily, "Will's got to be caught, Celia. This is the way."

"You mean you're helping Bide against us now?"

Sam said with stubborn anger, "I'm out to get Will Ballard, Celia. That's helping you more than Bide, if you only knew it."

Celia looked steadily at him, a strange hardness in her eyes. She said quietly,

"You're the man I'm going to marry, Sam. Is it right to ask you to clear these men out of here?"

There was a long, awkward pause, and Sam did not answer. Celia turned to the door behind her where Jim Young, his eyes grave and alert, was standing.

"Come along, Jim," she said quietly. "They want the house."

She brushed by Marriner and walked rapidly toward the bunkhouse. She heard Jim Young's step behind her, and she did not look back, and her thoughts were bitter and angry. Mel Young stood questioningly in the doorway, and she slipped past him and went over to Ike. He was still sleeping, and she sat in the chair beside him and stared wretchedly at the wall. She could hear the cook asleep in a far bunk, could hear Jim Young murmuring something to his brother, and an overwhelming feeling of despair was in her. She had tried to shame Sam into defending her and she had failed. It was Sam's stubborn pride that held him, and she knew every word he would use to her in justifying himself. He had always hated Will, and now that Will was proven a murderer in his eyes he would treat him as he would any killer. It was that simple to Sam, and he would not alter his opinion.

She heard the talk outside cease now, and surprisingly, then, Sam spoke, although she couldn't hear what he said. Presently Jim Young stepped into the room and clumsily started to tiptoe across to her.

She nodded, knowing that Sam had asked for her, and rose. For a moment there was an impulse in her to refuse, but she was afraid to. This meant so much to her, for she realized now the truth of the words she had used to shame Sam. She was going to marry him. She had promised him, and she would not make any man a wife if she didn't try to understand him.

Clinging to this, she went to the door and stepped outside and closed it behind her. The Young boys waited politely and stubbornly beside her, distrust of Sam in both their faces.

Sam said to the Youngs, "Go up to the house, you two."

Celia said, "It's all right," to them and then she started toward the cookshack. Sam fell in beside her, and when they were out of earshot of the brothers he said, "We've got to talk, Celia. Alone."

Celia said, "All right," and went over to the cookshack and stepped inside. The rough tables and benches, token of the old Hatchet, were still in their places. She sat on the closest bench and looked at Sam.

He nodded toward the house. "What happened up there?"

"Red Courteen."

"The Youngs said Ike was shot."

Celia said with sudden malice, "Odd—isn't it?—that a man would fight for his own people."

Sam said heavily, warningly, "Look, Celia. We've got to get this settled."

"It's all settled in my mind," Celia said levelly. "I'll listen to you, though."

Sam made an angry, savage gesture with his fist. "Good God, you'd think I was in the wrong, instead of Will Ballard!" His breathing was heavy, quick. "You're proud of Will—a damned killer!"

Celia said patiently, "Nobody's proud of killing, Sam. But I'm proud that Will wouldn't let John's killer go unpunished. I'm proud that Joe Kneen wouldn't too."

"Look at it!" Sam said angrily. "A sheriff, sworn on oath to uphold the law, turning over a prisoner to be butchered!"

"Will gave him a chance," Celia said quickly.

"How do you know?"

"I know Will."

Sam's face was ugly now as he regarded Celia. He stood in front of her, legs widespread, his big hands fisted at his sides. He took a deep breath and exhaled it shudderingly, as if in some way he knew the act could restrain his temper. But he could not hide it, and it was in his voice, making it rough and impatient and harsh.

He said slowly, "A year ago, Celia, I asked you to marry me and you said you would."

Celia didn't speak.

"I don't know much about women," Sam went on doggedly, "but I know what I want in a wife." He paused. "I want her to be loyal and I want her to believe in me and in what I do. Is that too much?"

"It's not too much, Sam."

Sam hesitated and then said it: "Are you being loyal? Do you believe in anything I do—anything?"

Celia said quietly, "No," and looked at him. She saw the shock in his face, and she knew that even now it wasn't too late. She could give in, and Sam would forgive her. All she needed to do was say she was sorry, and yet she couldn't make herself. She wasn't sorry, and she didn't believe in him, and she could sit here and calmly think that and wait to see what he did and feel proud.

For perhaps a minute Sam regarded her, and Celia knew what was in his mind as he watched her.

Then he said with surprising gentleness, "It wouldn't work, would it, Celia?"

Celia shook her head in negation.

"Too much Will Ballard," Sam murmured.

Celia shook her head. "Too much Sam Danfelser."

"No," Sam said, his tone tentative, as if he were just discovering something. "It's not me. It's Will. He's got a way about him. You can walk in a barroom and you know he's in it before you see him. You see a happy-looking girl at a dance, and you know Will has just left her." He looked closely at Celia now. "Bide showed me the tracks of Will's horse this morning where he'd met Ray. You were right, Celia. He gave Ray a gun and a chance at him, and he rode him down and killed him."

Celia didn't speak, and Sam went on in

the same voice, "He beat me up and did a job of it. And now he's taken you."

He paused, and Celia was almost afraid of the ugliness in his face. "I hate him, Celia," Sam said quietly. "I'm going to kill him."

He turned away from her and started for the doorway. He was almost through it when he halted abruptly, then dodged back into the room. He drew his gun and moved over to the window.

Then he turned to Celia and smiled crookedly and looked out the window again.

Celia moved slowly toward him. Over his shoulder she could see a spring wagon and team and a horseman. Will was driving the spring wagon, and his horse was tied to its tail gate. The horseman was a Mexican, and he was carrying a shovel across his saddle. The burden in the wagon was a new pine box, and Celia knew that it held the body of John Evarts.

Celia swiveled her head and glanced out the door. The ten horses in front of the house were gone, and she knew certainly that they had been hidden behind the house. Will had walked into their trap, and they were waiting for him.

Celia didn't wait. She streaked out the

door and headed at a dead run toward the wagon approaching the corral.

She heard Sam's sharp "Celia! Come back here!" and then his cursing and the heavy pounding of his feet as he came after her.

Celia ran desperately and heard Sam drawing closer, and then she yelled with all her might: "Will, get away! Ride off! Ride off!"

She saw Will yank on the reins at the sound of her voice and stand up in the wagon, looking at her. And then the first shot came from some panicked Bib M man in the house, and she saw Will drop the reins, step over the box, untie his horse, slip into the saddle, and again look toward her. A half-dozen shots came from the house now, stirring up spurts of dust beside his horse, and then suddenly he wheeled his horse and put it into a run toward the east.

Celia kept running, and then she tripped and fell heavily to the ground. She saw Sam run past her and stop to empty his gun at Will. Already a pair of horsemen up in the cottonwoods thundered off in pursuit, but she watched Sam's broad back. Each time he shot he brought his gun down savagely, as if clubbing a man, as if the violence of his effort could somehow knock Will from the saddle.

Will was hidden now by a break in the land, and she saw Sam fumbling out the fresh shells from his belt. Suddenly the futility of shooting occurred to him, and he wheeled and started to race back for his horse.

And then he saw Celia and hauled up in front of her. His face was contorted with rage and hatred, and at sight of it Celia laughed. She didn't know why, but she laughed at him. Sam raised his hand and slapped her across the face with his heavy hand, and she fell.

A pair of horsemen pounded past them, but Sam stood above her, staring at her, his mouth open a little in surprise at what he had done.

Celia raised a hand to her face and said quietly, "Thank you for that, Sam."

Sam hesitated only a second, and then he started to run for his horse, and Celia watching him, wondered if he would ever understand why she had thanked him.

Chapter 15

Lottie left her few purchases on the counter for her father to bring home later, said good night to the clerk, and left the store. She was glad for the cover of the night and had waited for it before she left the house. That way there was less chance that she might encounter other women, the mothers of the children she taught. For Lottie didn't know yet how she was going to face this. At noon the children had returned to school with something changed about them. They were excited and they whispered and they were restless. Lottie had seen this happen before, and she knew they would tell her in their own good time. It remained for little Tom Donovan to give it away after school. He stayed to ask her if Will had killed him with a shotgun.

That was the first Lottie knew of the killing of Ray Cavanaugh last night. The fact that it came from an eight-year-old made Lottie hot with shame and anger. This was a hard country, and more than once she had tried to explain an incident of violence to these children and give it a plausibility that didn't exist to her, but never before had it come so close. Will had killed a man who was in care of the sheriff. It was less easy to explain Sheriff Kneen's part than Will's, and Lottie was sick with disgust and humiliation. And she was angry with herself for waiting until darkness to sneak out and shop, as if in some obscure way she herself were guilty.

When she passed the last store she took her hat off and let the cool wind blow through her pale hair. She had not talked to her father at the store, but when he came tonight he would tell her what the town thought. She could tell then what course to take with the children at school tomorrow, but whatever it would be, she knew what she felt: It was plain, sick horror.

Turning in the gate in the darkness, she shut it behind her and came up the graveled walk.

A voice spoke quietly out of the night, "Let me in ahead of you, Lottie."

It was Will, and he stood next to the maple tree so that he blended with the trunk. Lottie wanted to say a hundred things then, but she detected an urgency in Will's voice that made her hurry up the steps.

She followed Will through the dark house to the kitchen, where he lighted the lamp in the wall bracket. When he turned to her she put her hat on the table and said, "I know. They're after you."

"Are they in town?" Will asked swiftly.

Lottie said, "I suppose they're all over town, aren't they? Isn't anybody entitled to shoot at you now?"

Will's face altered a little as understanding came, but he said nothing.

Lottie said in a small voice, "How could you do it, Will?"

"I didn't like it," Will said curtly. "Let's don't talk about it, Lottie."

"What can I tell the children I teach? What can I tell myself?"

Will came over to her and put his hands on her upper arms, gripping them tightly. "I did what I had to do. Now let's don't talk about it, I say."

Quiet accusation was in every line of Lottie's face as she answered him. "It's not easy to live with murder, is it, Will?"

Anger flared in Will's eyes, and the line of his jaw was hard. He let his hands drop and turned away from her. Moving over to the window curtain, he looked out into the night and then let the curtain drop and said matter-of-factly, "I'm on the dodge, Lottie. Bide and Sam were waiting at Hatchet when I came in this afternoon with John's body. It took me till dark to shake them and their crew."

"Do you want to hide here?" Lottie asked quietly. "Won't they look here first?"

Will said shortly, "I'm not staying." He came slowly, hesitantly, over to her. "I came because I didn't want to leave things the way they are between us, Lottie." He added somberly, "It looks like they aren't the same. They're worse."

"And whose fault is it?"

Will shook his head wearily and sighed. "Lottie, go see Joe Kneen. You respect him. Ask him how it happened. Ask him why. I haven't the time to make it plain."

"Joe Kneen's as guilty as you are."

Will nodded. "Exactly as guilty."

They were standing just as they had stood that morning they had almost quarreled, the expression on their faces exactly the same, and Lottie almost wondered if time hadn't stood still, if everything that had happened these past few days had not been a dream.

She said bitterly, "I promised you once that right or wrong I would help you if you needed me. What do you need, Will? Food? Blankets? Guns?"

"Nothing—when it's offered that way."

Lottie said passionately, "But, Will, it's so useless to keep this up! You're getting over your head! And for what? Bide's still on Hatchet! Sam's hunting you! One of your men is shot! The cattle you've taken are gone! Celia isn't able to——" She paused, seeing the surprise wash over Will's face. She said then, "Didn't you know? Red Courteen took all the cattle from Hatchet's pasture yesterday."

Will said quietly, "Courteen? His weren't there."

A faint flush crept into Lottie's face. "Dad sold him his cattle. Red went in to take them, and one of your men was hurt in the fight."

Will's eyes were dark, somber, watchful, and Lottie had to steel herself to face what she saw in them. Will said mildly then,

"You like that, don't you, Lottie?"

"Dad had a right to sell them! More right than you had to take them!"

Will nodded. "Trouble is, his nose for a dollar is pushing him into some peculiar company. You know Red, Lottie?"

Lottie didn't answer, and Will continued, his voice taking on a faint edge, "Red's number is coming up, Lottie. Tell your father it's coming up for anybody that runs with Red too."

Still Lottie didn't answer. Will said, "Who was hurt?"

"Ike Adams, I think."

Will turned away from her and went over to the stove and gathered up a handful of matches and put them in his shirt pocket. Then he went to the back door and stood by it and said mildly, "One of us has got to change, Lottie. I can't. I can meet you over on the reservation in two days, and we can have the preacher marry us. But that wouldn't change me. I'd come back to Hatchet."

"And I'll meet you on the reservation in two days and marry you, Will. But if you come back to Hatchet you'll never see me again."

They looked long at each other, and Will said gently, "You see? One of us has got to change."

"I see it." Lottie couldn't keep the quaver out of her voice.

And neither of them in their pride would move a step toward the other. They both waited, hoping the other would break, but it was Lottie who knew neither of them would.

Will saw it in her face, and he said in a discouraged voice, "I figured I'd come and go from Cavanaugh's place while they're hunting me, Lottie. I'll be there two nights from now. If you change your mind ride up to it and we'll go over to the reservation. Will you do that?"

"If I change my mind," Lottie said quietly.

Will glanced briefly, almost hungrily, at her and then slipped out of the doorway into the night.

Chapter 16

Around eight o'clock in the morning, when most of Boundary was on the street, Bide Marriner and Sam Danfelser with their crews rode into town. It was an imposing aggregation of riders, and people stopped to watch them, knowing vaguely that this was connected in some way with the shooting of Ray Cavanaugh.

The riders dismounted in front of the Belle Fourche, and a few of them loafed around the steps of the saloon while others, among them Bide and Sam, went inside. The Belle Fourche, in this last week, had become more of a clearing-house of information than ever. It was here that the men from the outfits under Indian Ridge waited, nursing their small poker games along, for news of the fortunes of Hatchet or Bib M.

Bide and Sam had timed their entrance shrewdly this morning. A whole day had passed since Cavanaugh was killed, allowing time for the news of it to spread to Indian Ridge and draw the small outfits to town.

As Bide and Sam entered the Belle Fourche this morning Bide grunted with satisfaction at what he saw. There were four or five of the Ridge ranchers here, along with a couple from the Indigos.

Bide was too shrewd a man to beat a drum. He and Sam bellied up to the bar and asked for beers and spoke to acquaintances. Schultz came in with a box of forty-five shells, and Bide put his shell belt on the bar and began to fill it with fresh cartridges.

Harve Garretson came up and said, "Seen Joe Kneen?" and Bide said he hadn't. A couple of the Ridge ranchers came up behind Garretson to listen.

"What's he doin'?" Bide asked idly, fingering the smooth cartridges into his worn belt.

"Nothin', far as anybody knows."

"Joe," Bide observed mildly, "has resigned, only he don't know it."

Garretson regarded him worriedly. "You think he will?"

"Resign?" There was scorn in Bide's voice, but he went on with his loading. "He don't have to. Any man that pays any attention to Joe from now on is a fool."

Another pair of Ridge ranchers drifted up. They were a taciturn, footless lot, and Marriner knew they disliked and envied him and that his hold on them was slight. But he was wise enough to treat them as equals, for he had been one of them himself once. In those days Phil Evarts considered him half rustler, half clown, and Bide could date his hatred of Evarts from those days. He was not going to make the same mistake himself, for these men, with their endless cousins, their crews, could catch Will for him.

Garretson said, still worried, "It don't look right. Him sittin' there and Ballard on the loose."

Sam spoke for the first time. "You know what to do about that, don't you?" When Garretson didn't answer Sam said grimly, "The same thing I'm doin'."

Bide let a note of sarcasm creep into his voice now. "This isn't a club, Harve. You can join it without payin' dues."

"What?"

Bide's speech again was careless. "A bunch of us aim to do Joe's job for him, since he won't. We're going to get Will

Ballard." He went on loading his belt, waiting for a reply, and there was only silence. He looked up at Garretson, in whose face was only a very mild interest tempered with caution. Shuttling his glance to the Ridge riders, he saw the same thing. Exasperation edged into Bide's thin face, and he said tauntingly, "If you're gettin' too old, Harve, send your men."

Garretson shook his head. "I don't reckon. That's Joe's job."

Bide ceased his work, wrath building up in his voice. "And he's doin' it, is he?"

"No. But I don't want any of it."

"Will got your cattle, didn't he?"

"All right," Garretson murmured. "I've got 'em back and sold 'em. I'm out of it."

Again Bide glanced at the others. Whatever judgment they had about this they were reserving, and Bide, in whom aggressiveness would not be subdued, said truculently to the lot of them, "What about you fellows?"

"Oh, we're all together," Garretson said. "We been talkin' it over this mornin'." He paused. "It ain't our fight."

"But you'll take Hatchet grass when Will's licked, won't you?"

"You got to lick him first," one man pointed out.

Bide's angry glance almost pounced on him. "I'll lick him—with your help or without it!" He looked around at the men and then at Garretson, and he said angrily, "What's bitin' you boys? Are you scared of him?"

"That's right," Garretson said mildly.

Bide just stared, his mouth open a little. It was incomprehensible to him that any man could admit this. He looked wonderingly at Sam and found the same puzzlement in his face. He turned again to Garretson and said blankly, "Well, why?"

Garretson said dryly, "I'm no hand with a gun, Bide—never claimed to be. I'd just breathe a heap easier without that Injun on my neck. So damned if I'll hunt him or take his grass."

By this time most of the barroom had gathered around Bide and Garretson, and Bide looked the crowd over in one bitter, sweeping glance. He said violently, "Well, what in the hell did you think he'd do when you first decided to move in? Not fight you?"

Nobody spoke for a moment, and then a

man at the outside of the crowd said, "You missed him yesterday, Bide, so your crew says. He's loose and warned. He don't forget."

Sam's flat palm crashed down on the bar top with the violence of a pistol report. "He's only a man!" He said wrathfully, challengingly, and there was again silence.

Garretson murmured dryly, "That's right. He whittled you down a couple of inches, though, didn't he?"

Sam brushed Bide out of the way with a sweep of his arm, sending him roughly into the men beside him. He came up to Garretson, his bruised face ugly with a passionate anger.

"He did, by God! And I'll kill him for it!" He looked around with a hard and bitter arrogance. "And when I do, I won't need any of you yellow-bellies to hold him for me!"

He roughly pushed his way through the half circle of men and tramped out, his step booming heavily on the saloon floor. There was a long moment of silence as these men looked at each other in surprise.

Bide picked his shell belt off the bar and strapped it on and said, "The more of us there are, the quicker the job's done. Let's go."

He strode through the crowd which was breaking up and paused on the steps. Sam was just stepping into the saddle, and Bide walked over to him and stood by him.

"That ain't any way to get up a bunch," he said, mild accusation in his voice.

"They wouldn't come out anyhow," Sam said shortly.

"I know, but we need 'em behind us. What do——?"

"Damn it, Bide, what are we waiting for?" Sam's voice overrode Bide's in its quivering wrath.

Bide regarded him in utter surprise, and then he said placatingly, "What are we?" and turned to his horse.

Celia, dismounting in front of the courthouse, saw the posse pass, headed south. Afterward she went to Kneen's office and, finding the door open, knocked on the jamb and stepped inside.

She surprised Kneen sitting with his feet on the desk, staring dreamily at the wall. He came to his feet hurriedly, but his face for a moment held the sadness of his thoughts.

He pulled up a chair for her and then sat down again, and she noticed that in some way he had changed since she last saw him. He was at once less worried and sadder than she remembered him, and she smiled at him. "I didn't think you'd be with them."

"Bide?" Kneen smiled faintly. "No. That's their own idea, I'm afraid."

Celia said, "I heard about it from—from Sam. Not much. Can you tell me how it happened?"

In his tired voice Kneen told her of the message he had sent to Will by Jim Young and told her why, too. His story of the shooting was factual, emotionless, and he watched her closely as he told it. At the finish of it Celia said gently, "They blame you, too, don't they?"

Kneen nodded and grimaced wryly. "There's nothing they can do about it."

"What happens now?" Celia asked.

Kneen said soberly, "I wish I knew. I'm only sure of one thing." He shook his head. "I can't help you now. The town's against me. They call it murder. Bide and Sam have taken over the duties of my office, and they can do pretty much what they like."

"Will's left."

"On the dodge, I reckon," Kneen said bitterly. "I haven't heard that the new sheriffs have put a price on his head, but that'll come."

Celia was motionless, and Kneen said quietly, "This is none of my business, Celia. But can't you talk to Sam?"

"I'm no more to Sam now than any other girl," Celia answered.

Kneen's gaze dropped, and Celia stood up. "There's just one thing more I wanted to ask you. I want you to tell me the truth and forget Will's worked for us all this time." At Kneen's nod she asked earnestly, watching him with narrow attention. "In your heart do you think Will did wrong?"

Kneen said immediately, "No. It was the only way."

Celia smiled. "That makes three of us," she said and bid him good-by and went out.

At her horse Celia knew she hadn't asked the questions of Kneen that she wanted to, and she realized miserably that he couldn't have answered them if she had. One of them had been answered when she saw the posse riding out this morning, and she knew Will had escaped yesterday. The other one—how long he could dodge them—probably nobody could answer, and yet she had to know.

She had dismounted in front of Priest's Emporium before she realized the significance of what she was about to do. Priest was one of Hatchet's enemies now. Celia thought about it a moment and then sensibly decided to go in.

Priest, however, thought differently. When he saw her enter he promptly found an errand in the rear of the store. Celia made her few purchases and went out, but the memory of Priest disturbed her. And thinking of him, she thought of Lottie, and the thought was so startling that she halted in the middle of the sidewalk. Then she mounted and put her horse downstreet until she was almost to the edge of the town. She could see the schoolyard now, with the children romping at morning recess.

Celia went on and dismounted in the yard and saw Lottie Priest interrupt her play with the smallest children to stare at her. Celia's resolution almost failed her now that she was here, but she went on toward Lottie, saying hello to the children she knew.

Lottie came over to her, wearing a dark coat thrown over her shoulders. *She's pretty*, Celia thought, and she forgave the coolness in Lottie's eyes as Lottie spoke to her.

"Can't we——?" Celia looked at the children ringed around watching them. Lottie shooed the children off and led the way into the schoolroom. It was bright and tidy like Lottie herself, Celia thought as she followed Lottie up front and took the chair Lottie offered her.

Lottie sat behind her desk, and Celia had a fleeting moment of discomfort. She had known Lottie for years; they had been to the same dances and knew the same men, and yet Lottie was a town girl, Celia a cattleman's daughter, and their lives were not alike. There was little in common between them, except Will, and Celia was uncomfortably aware of that now. She found nothing to talk about now except what she had come for, and it was like her not to hesitate.

"I wondered if you know where Will is?" Celia asked. "I knew he would see you first if he could."

"Yes, he saw me," Lottie said in a kind of toneless, pleasant voice. "He said he'd be at Cavanaugh's shack under Indian Ridge night after next."

"Is he—was he all right when you saw him?"

Lottie's eyes were cool with dislike, and she said in the same neutral voice, "He wasn't hurt."

Celia had learned everything she wanted, and yet parting like this wasn't right. This was the girl Will was going to marry, and she herself was Will's friend. Will seldom mentioned Lottie, but Celia had sensed long ago that he and Lottie were not agreed on Hatchet's course. But Will was in trouble now, and it seemed to Celia that anyone who was Will's friend now should deserve Lottie's friendliness too. And it was not here.

Celia said in a kindly voice, "Don't worry about him, Lottie. It will all come out somehow."

"Those are fine words," Lottie said with quiet bitterness. "They don't happen to mean anything, though."

"You don't believe Will can be caught, do you?"

"Doesn't he deserve to be?" Lottie countered. "He murdered a man."

Celia said quietly, "You want him to be, you mean?"

"You know it's not what I mean," Lottie said quickly. "The harm is done—to him. Catching him doesn't count."

"I think you're wrong," Celia said quietly.

Lottie's eyes were bright with fleeting anger. "I know you do. You and Will have always thought alike when Hatchet has something to gain."

Celia looked at her curiously, pitying her, not wholly understanding her either. She saw something then that she had not suspected before, and she said almost with astonishment, "You hate me, Lottie. I never understood that before. You do, don't you?"

"Only because you're part of Hatchet," Lottie said in quiet bitterness. "You—all of you—have turned Will into something he isn't—until now he can murder a man."

"Sam says Will changed me," Celia murmured.

"Maybe Sam's right. You're both the same kind, whoever was changed."

Celia, regarding her gravely, murmured, "That's the nicest thing I've had said of me."

She stood up now, but Lottie did not move. "I'd hate to have it said of me,"

Lottie said with quiet passion.

"Lottie!" Celia's voice was appalled. "Do you know what you're saying?"

"Yes."

There was a defiant and bitter disillusion in Lottie's eyes for a moment, and then she stood up too. "Go up and see him," she said in that toneless, pleasant voice. "Will you tell him something for me when you go?"

Celia nodded mutely.

"Tell him I'm not coming up. He'll understand. Just tell him that."

Chapter 17

From the hill above Bib M Will watched Bide's ranch outfit come awake to a spring morning. He saw the first fire lighted, the pair of horse wranglers leave in the half-light to bring in the horses, and, remembering Bide's impatience, he smiled. Bide had missed him yesterday by the narrowest of margins. Two minutes later and Will's horse would have been turned into the corral, leaving him afoot for Bide to corner. Celia had prevented that, and again Will wondered what had happened there afterward. Bide had always been a little afraid of all the Evarts, but in anger he was dangerous. Sam, whatever he thought of Celia's actions, would have held Bide in check, though, and that was Will's lone comfort.

The house on the ugly bald hill below him slowly took shape in the increasing light, and Will, shivering a little, settled back in patience. He had traveled most of the night to reach the spot back in the Salt Hills where he had spent two cold wakeful hours trying to sleep until he moved again before dawn.

Bide's crew lived and ate in the big house with him, and they all left it at the same time for the corral below when breakfast was finished. Each carried a bedroll. Will counted them and judged that Bide had pulled some of his crew from the herd at Russian Springs. They saddled up and moved off in pairs, loafing down the valley, until the last man, putting his horse into a lope to catch up with the others, was away. Then they bunched and rode out smartly, Bide and Russ Schultz heading them, and Will turned his attention to the house.

He shifted farther down the slope, so that the porch was brought in his line of vision, and waited, watchful. Nothing stirred around Bib M, and presently Will came down the slope to the rear of the house and quietly skirted it and came onto the porch.

Again he stopped to listen and heard nothing and went through the nearest door, which was open. This was the L that contained the bunk room. Its dark closeness held a litter of clothes and gear and smelled of leather and sweat and wool. Will moved silently, alertly, through the room to a connecting door and stood in it, looking at the clean long table here and beyond it into the kitchen lean-to, which was also deserted. That left another room, and he went over and peered into Bide's office and, seeing it empty, came back into the lean-to that was the kitchen. The cook, apparently, had been the last man to leave, for the lean-to was cleaned up as if the crew expected to be gone some time.

Will went through the supplies stacked in a corner shelf and found food he wanted. He had to hunt some time for a coffeepot small enough to carry, but he found a battered one without a top that had seen hard service. Afterward he went back to the bunk room and found a pair of tattered blankets. His own outfit had been in the wagon with the coffin when Bide surprised him, and last night he had been too proud to ask anything of Lottie.

Before he left Will laid a coin on Bide's desk in payment. He was certain Bide would not miss these things or be curious about the money, but leaving it gave him an obscure satisfaction.

Later, at full sunup, he found his horse and put him south toward D Cross. There were things he wanted to see now before the hunt got close to him, and this might be his last chance.

He clung to the trails threading the open timber of the Salt Hills most of that day until he was far south of Six X, and then he swung down through the foothills and camped that night on the edge of the flats. He could risk a fire for another night, he judged. He ate Bib M grub and afterward, a blanket wrapped around him against the chill that was still in the spring night, heard the train from Boundary hooting for the grade way station far to the south of him.

He chucked a stick on the fire now and, with the sound still in his ears, remembered the times he had heard it before, always feeling the pull it had for every fiddle-footed man. The pull was not there for him tonight, and he felt the irony of it. Tonight, for the first time in years, he was free to drift, and no man would blame him. Always before there was Lottie to hold him. But in these last days that hold had loosened and fallen away. He knew it was gone and he did not understand fully how it came about, but he knew that he would wait out tomorrow night at Cavanaugh's shack with only a faint hope in him and find himself alone at daylight. A man lost most things that way, not by a violent wrenching, but by a slow dissolution. Hatchet had faded that way, and now Lottie was lost to him the same way, and when it had started he did not know. His mind and his heart had been closing against Lottie, and hers had been closing against him until the course of their lives hung on a show of their obstinacy. The thought of it had the power to make him sad, but that was all. Lottie was gone, and he was free to drift, and yet he did not want to.

Somewhere back in the hills a coyote with her pups paused to shout at the stars, and Will laughed, his mood shattered. Rising, he went out to move his picket pin and put his horse on new grass and afterward came back and moved his blankets away from the fire and rolled into them.

Before he slept his thoughts drifted back to Hatchet and to Celia. Hers was the gray duty of burying John Evarts and he tried to picture it and failed. There was Sam to ease that for her, but afterward what was there for her?

Sam was against her and against him, and yet she was trying to keep them both. She could not, Will knew, and he accepted the fact that someday, maybe soon, too, she would tell him to go. He did not think of that, because of all his thoughts, this was the least welcome. Presently he slept.

Long before there was light in the sky Will was riding again, this time north, edging away from the Salt Hills onto the range of Six X.

The order of these holdings was in his mind. Case at Six X and Ladder and Sam Danfelser and Bide Marriner held the range of the Salt Hills and the flats below them in that order, moving south to north. All of these outfits had for their main source of water Bandoleer Creek, which came out of the Salt Hills on Bide's range and swung south, angling out into the flats and finally touching Boundary and again swinging on south.

Beyond Bandoleer Creek to the west, approaching Hatchet range, water was less easy to find, and it was through this country that Will rode today. The winter's heavy snows had brought up a thick grass here, and Will was reminded of Phil Evarts. This stretch of range that lay between the Salt Hills outfits and the edge of Hatchet had always tantalized Phil Evarts, perhaps only because it marked the limit beyond which he could not extend Hatchet's holdings. No man stopped him; it was nature, for this stretch was waterless. The cattle from Hatchet grazed out into it, but they must always return for water. Likewise, cattle from the Salt Hills ranches edged into it but drifted back to Bandoleer Creek for water. Until Bide Marriner developed Russian Springs, that was. Following which, of course, Phil Evarts took it away from him. For outside of the two wells that Phil Evarts had dug and which were failures, Russian Springs was the only water in this stretch which was claimed for Hatchet.

In the early morning Will came upon the first Six X cattle pushed out by Case. The recent rains and the new grass allowed them to graze deep into this strip, and Will was not surprised.

And then in midmorning he came upon the first D Cross cattle. A scattering of them was gathered at one of Phil Evarts' dug wells and was watched by a pair of D Cross riders, dismounted and having a smoke.

Will pulled his horse back into the coulee he had just left and moved, afoot now, closer in the deep grass until he could make out the brands on more of the cattle.

It was D Cross all right. He came back to his horse and made a wide circle of the well, but he was disturbed. This was claimed as Hatchet range, and Sam Danfelser's cattle were on it. Sam was not the man to do this behind Celia's back. Or had he despaired of Celia ever moving off the others and decided to claim his share of Hatchet to save it from falling to Marriner or Case? Will wished savagely that he could see Celia now and find out.

Keeping on north now, holding to cover where it was afforded, he came into the range around Russian Springs in the afternoon. The country here was different, more broken, and rolling, long patches of timber darkly stippling the new green of the grass. There were cattle all through it, and Bide's Bib M brand was on them.

Will moved deeper into this country, for he had measured his risk. Bide would have pulled most of his men off to hunt him, yet Will moved carefully, keeping to the timber and the high ground until, some hours later, he came upon the open valley where Russian Springs lay.

Russian Springs had got its name from a peddler who had been murdered years ago in his camp here by Indians coveting his trade goods. The Springs themselves were at the head of the valley, welling up under at the base of a towering outcrop of rotten limestone. A big tank had been rocked up under the base to hold the water, and its overflow, filtering down the valley floor, left a stripe of deeper green the length of it. Across the valley were the log shack and corrals which Bide had thrown up originally, only to lose to Phil Evarts and now regain.

Will noted the horses in the far corral and saw a pair of Bide's hands yarning in the sun outside, but he paid them scant attention. It was the springs themselves that interested him, and he studied them closely for many minutes.

Afterward he pulled away from the valley and again kept north and by full dark was in the foothills of the Indian Ridge country.

More cautious now, when he came to a stream he rested his horse and had some cold grub and a cigarette and afterward climbed to one of the many trails that threaded a way to the Ridge and the Cavanaugh shack.

He traveled this timbered terrain carefully, his senses alert now, for he was in the country where Bide would naturally hunt him. But with him now, too, was a melancholy he could not shake. Later tonight he would make the shack and his answer from Lottie would be waiting there. He thought of her now, and little things about her, lovable things, rose to taunt him.

He reined up suddenly, hardly knowing why. There was the smell of wood smoke plain in the forest air, and he felt his horse uneasy under him. Suddenly, ahead of him and not far distant, a horse nickered sharply.

Will rolled out of the saddle instantly and lunged for his black's head, covering its nose with his hand to prevent an answering whicker. He listened, then, and heard men talking, and he pulled his horse around and led him quietly back down the trail. He heard now the sudden pounding of horses at a dead run behind him. Vaulting into the saddle, he roweled his horse off the trail some twenty yards into thick brush and again dismounted, again covered his horse's nose with his hand. Seconds later a pair of riders he could not see pounded past on the dark trail at a reckless speed.

Will mounted and returned to the trail and turned up it, lifting his horse into a run. There was a chance that other men were ahead, but he determined to risk it. He came over a rise and saw the small campfire by the trail, bedrolls beside it. The camp was empty, and he kept his horse at a dead run through it and stopped only minutes later far beyond to blow his horse and listen. The night was quiet once more, but Will listened with an uneasiness upon him. His idle time was up; Bide's men were riding the hills, watching the trails already. From now on it was travel hard, keep moving, and forget sleep.

He pressed on, sobered now and alert, moving deeper into the gaunt canyons and steep timber of Indian Ridge. Later in the night then he paused on the canyon rim overlooking the trail down into Cavanaugh's place. If there was a light in the shack he would see it.

He moved down the steep trail and presently came into the clearing around the shack. He approached it carefully and found it empty, just as he had left it.

He put his horse behind the shack, returned and stretched out on the porch, and presently slept.

He awoke sometime later, dismay in him. He did not move, only listened. And then there came to him the sound of a horse being ridden down the trail, and he knew this had wakened him. A fierce joy was in him, and he came to his feet, peering into the darkness. This was Lottie.

The rider came on and was now abreast of the well. Will listened intently, and then he caught the rustle of cloth and he stepped down and said, "You came, Lottie."

The rider stopped, and there was no answer. Will halted, and his hand dropped to his gun, in case he had made a mistake.

And then the answer came. "It's me, Will—Celia."

Will felt the hope in him die, leaving a sharp, brief bitterness. That was all, and he came up to Celia's horse. "You've seen Lottie."

"She said she wasn't coming, Will."

"I didn't mean that," Will said sharply, and then he realized that Celia wouldn't know what he was talking about. "I only wondered how you found me."

"Yes, she told me."

Will silently thought of this. Lottie was

gone, and she had not troubled to tell him herself. Will knew that was unfair. They had said everything there was to say long ago, and she had ended it with bitterness and accusation.

Will was suddenly aware that Celia was silent, watching him. He told her to dismount and took her horse and put it with his own.

He went over to Cavanaugh's woodpile now and picked up some chips and chunks of wood and brought them over close to the porch and built a fire. He watched it come alight, a taciturn expression on his still face, and presently he looked up at Celia, who sat on the edge of the porch. He found her looking at him curiously, uncertainly, like a sober child.

"Would you rather I hadn't come, Will?"

Will rose and said gently, "I was never more glad to see you," and his smile was quick, careless.

"Isn't this fire risky?" she asked.

Will nodded soberly and looked at her and again grinned. "It is."

Celia laughed suddenly, for the first time in days. She could forget now that she had watched John Evarts buried this morning in the hills behind Hatchet alongside her father, his brother. She was with Will again, and that dry, blunt, truth-telling, humorous part of him hadn't changed. It was like being home. Will sat beside her now and began to fashion a cigarette. He said idly, "Tell me about Lottie."

When Celia didn't answer he looked at her and saw the soberness in her eyes. "I'd rather not," Celia said slowly.

Will watched her a moment, understanding, and then he looked away. "It doesn't matter. If she'd come here tonight we'd have ridden over to the reservation and been married. But she didn't come."

"What was it, Will?"

"Hatchet."

Celia said quietly after a moment, "I think I know how you feel—a little." When he glanced at her she said, "Sam's not going to marry me, Will. He told me."

Will looked at her sharply, an unaccountable gladness in his eyes. It took a moment for him to accept the fact that this gay and courageous daughter of Phil Evarts was not going to marry a man who didn't deserve her. He studied her dark face, her gray, musing eyes, and he saw no heartbreak there and he said quietly, "Bless him. He finally saw you weren't good enough for him, did he?"

Celia glanced quickly at him and saw the humor and friendliness in his eyes and understood the meaning behind his words. She nodded, smiling.

Will tossed his unmade cigarette in the fire and said soberly, "I told you, kid. We're mavericks. This was in the book."

"For you and Lottie too?"

Will nodded. "That was in the books. I didn't have the sense to see it."

"But if it hadn't been for Hatchet maybe—"

"It would have been something else and too late, then. She wants it safe."

Celia, listening, nodded. "Sam does too."

They looked at each other fully now, and suddenly Will shook his head. "Peace be with them, then."

They were quiet a moment, both staring at the fire, a closeness between them that did not need speech. Celia said suddenly, in a small voice, "I guess it isn't wrong to say it now, Will. But when Sam told me I felt as if a door opened." She looked at him with quiet wonder in her eyes. "I'd been in the dark. I didn't know it." She hesitated. "You knew I was, Will, and you didn't tell me."

"One man's opinion," Will said, smiling gently.

Celia sighed deeply and shook her head. "I'm afraid of him. He believes in the right things and he's honest, but there's a wild streak in him, Will. Not a wild streak like yours. I—I can understand yours. You don't think you're better than other men; you just think the things you believe are better than what other men believe. But that's not Sam's wildness." She shivered a little. "He thinks he was born in the right. He only believes in himself and he'll break and smash everything in front of him to prove it to himself. He—he thinks he's God, almost."

Will listened, watching her, knowing this was something she had to rid her mind of. Beneath it, now, he saw the shape of fear, and it puzzled him. He said gently, "Sam's trouble is he hates to take a beating."

"He hates it most from you," Celia murmured.

Will shook his head. "From anybody."

"But most from you," Celia repeated. "He's going to kill you, Will. He told me."

Will didn't smile. He asked suddenly, "Is

that what you're afraid of, Celia?"

Celia nodded. "That's why I came, I guess. I didn't know why I did come—until I said that."

Will's glance shuttled to the fire, and he stared at it a long time, his face settling into a tough-shaped somberness. He said gently, "I can promise you one thing, Celia. Sam won't get a chance to kill me until Hatchet is on its feet again."

Celia laughed uncertainly. "That's as good as forever, Will."

He glanced at her levelly. "I don't think so."

"We've got two hands, a cook, a cripple, and a foreman on the dodge. Aren't you just wishing, Will?"

"There's a way," Will said quietly. "See what you think of it."

He rose and got some more wood and threw it on the fire, and afterward he talked long into the night.

Chapter 18

This amused Joe Kneen, and he watched it with a dry and bitter relish. At all hours of the day and night tired riders drifted into town. They would report to Sam and Bide at the Belle Fourche when those two were in, which was seldom, and then cross to the hotel and sleep like the dead in the rooms Bide had engaged for them. The town watched and heard stories. There was the one about Will passing two D Cross riders on a trail at night, and they had tracked him up into the Indian Ridge where they found his fire still warm in the mouth of a cave. They had called in help and had spent a futile day beating the brush, and afterward the original two had gone back to their old camp. They found a warm fire, their bedrolls burned, their grub vanished, and a coin left prominently on a rock.

Then there was the time—yesterday, that

was—when two riders, their horses lathered, rode into Boundary, each from a different direction, each swearing that they had seen Will Ballard ride through the piece of country they were watching.

Late one night, too, one of Garretson's hands was brought into Boundary in a spring wagon. He had jumped Will Ballard in the Indigos and, heedless of his employer's decision that his outfit had no part in this, had tried an ambush. The doctor said he had a good chance to live.

Kneen heard all this at second hand, usually relayed to him by one of the ranchers from under the Ridge, who still sat by and watched. Which was what Kneen was doing, too, this morning, as he had every morning since the shooting of Cavanaugh.

He opened his office around seven-thirty, took care of whatever business the town and county chose to bring to him, and then waited, while out in the hills Bide Marriner and Sam Danfelser drove their men and horses to exhaustion trying to find a man they would kill on sight.

This morning Kneen picked up his mail at the post office and brought it back to the courthouse and was leafing through the new *Stockman's Gazette* when Lowell Priest and Red Courteen came into his office. Kneen threw the *Gazette* on the desk and bid them good morning.

Priest answered him with bare civility. Red Courteen put his shoulder against the wall and watched.

"Kneen," Priest said truculently, 'I was robbed last night."

"A holdup?" Kneen inquired mildly.

"No. My store. It was broken into sometime in the night."

Kneen gestured toward a chair and said, "Sit down and tell me about it. What's gone?"

"Powder," Priest said curtly.

Kneen tried to suppress a smile, but he was not quite successful. The irritability in Priest's thin, precise face deepened, and he said sharply, "What's funny about that, Kneen?"

"Nothing," Kneen drawled. "I just figured whoever took it couldn't hide it forever."

"There's a sledge and pipe gone too."

"All right."

Priest said sharply, "Aren't you going to have a look?"

"They're gone, aren't they?" Kneen drawled. "Somebody pried off that dollar padlock on your lean-to and helped themselves. Isn't that it?"

Priest just glared at him, and Kneen went on in the same mild, prodding voice, "I told you ten times, Priest, to move that powder or else store it where fire couldn't get at it. Each time you told me you were moving it next week. Maybe"—his voice was dry, thrusting—"some of your neighbors who didn't want their stores blown to hell moved it for you."

Color crept into Priest's sallow face, and he was silent. Red Courteen moved away from the wall and said mildly, "Maybe you did it yourself, Joe."

Kneen looked at Courteen for a long, speculative moment and then spat elaborately.

Red's tough face darkened with anger, and he came over to stand beside Priest. Kneen looked at the storekeeper and said with calculated insolence, "What's he doing here? A witness?"

"No. He——"

"Then get out of here, Red," Kneen said with a deceptive mildness, coming out of his chair.

"Wait, Kneen!" Priest said sharply.

Kneen looked at him questioningly, and there was fight in his pale eyes. Priest said, "We're—uh—business partners. He has a right to be here."

Kneen said blankly, "In the store?"

"We're running cattle together," Priest said uncomfortably. When Kneen kept staring at him Priest said, "I bought out Garretson's share of that herd, and Red's running them for me."

"Where?"

Priest hesitated. "Just east of Garretson's."

Which was a mealymouthed way of saying Hatchet, Kneen knew, and he looked from one to the other, and then he said in a tired voice as if to himself, "Oh, the hell with it." He shouldered past them to the door and stood by it.

"Now get out, you pair of jackals! Get out!" The last words came in a shout.

Priest did not hesitate; he scuttled past him. Red walked with a stiff furious dignity, and Kneen slammed the door viciously on him.

He stood there a moment, so mad he was almost sick, and then he came back to his chair and sank into it. He knew what he should have done. He should have given them just one day to get off Hatchet. But there was Red's crew to deal with, and there was himself. In disgrace, unable to command help, all he could do was what the lowliest Indian Ridge rancher could do—wait the outcome of the hunt in the hills.

I've got to wait, he thought; he tried to make a refrain of it in his mind, but it was drowned in a torrent of inward bitter cursing.

Chapter 19

Will wakened at sunset and raised on his elbows, looking about him. For a long minute he flagged his sleep-drugged mind toward a memory of this place, which was a thick tangle of scrub oak by a stream in the lower slopes of the Indigos. He rose now, quietly as he could, and saw his horse grazing upstream, barely discernible in the fading light.

Rolling his blankets up, he moved toward the stream and knelt by it. The shock of the cold water brought him to wakefulness, and he drank, afterward looking about him again. This place looked like all the others where he had snatched a few hours of daylight sleep and rested his horse. It had taken an effort of will to remember the days, but he was certain that tomorrow morning was the one he had named to Celia.

He drank again, feeling the cold water

smother his hunger a little, and then rose and headed for his horse. These last days had fined down his face, which was blurred now by a thick black beard stubble. His leg muscles were iron-hard with saddle-stiffness as he walked, for, except when he stole these occasional hours of deep, exhausted sleep, he had not been out of the saddle.

He pulled up the picket rope, afterward stroking the coat of his black gelding and regarding him critically in the dusk. He was gaunted up, too, but there were no sores yet. Will slapped his rump and then took down his saddle blanket, which he had hung on a branch to dry in the afternoon sun.

Working the bumps out of it so that it would not gall, he rubbed it between his hands to take out the stiffness and afterward saddled up. By deep dusk he was riding again, this time out onto the flats toward the east, beyond Hatchet, to a rendezvous. He found he was not thinking of that, however; his mind kept returning to something he had seen yesterday. That was the day one of Garretson's hands had shot at him. He'd been riding down a trail to the north, half sleeping in his saddle, his mind drowsing and unawares, when his horse shied. He had been pitched from the saddle just as a gun went off some fifty feet in front of him. The man had come running toward him out of the brush, gun in hand, and Will had shot at him and hit him. Afterward he had carried the man down close to one of Garretson's line shacks on the flats because he had asked it.

Will had propped him against a tree, feeling only a pity for the man. He had looked around him and said, "You sure Harve will hear my shots?"

"Courteen will," the man whispered. "Him and his crew are running cattle over there. They'll hear you."

Will had shot into the air and left him. But the knowledge that Priest and Courteen had kept their cattle on Hatchet grass both puzzled and disturbed him. If Lottie had given her father Will's message, then Priest was either a fool or a brave man. And Will wanted to find out which—after tomorrow.

He rode steadily through the night now, his hunger becoming more and more insistent. The last of his grub had vanished yesterday, and there would be no more until morning.

He passed early in the night behind

Hatchet to the south and sometime in the night came close to the seep where the skeleton of Bide's chuck wagon still lay.

It was just breaking false dawn when he slanted into the shallow valley above Russian Springs and was hailed quietly from the timber.

He rode into the edge of it and saw first the team and spring wagon, and then Jim Young looked up in the darkness, Mel beside him.

Will said, "Got any cooked grub between you?" and laughed at himself; the sudden sound of his own voice almost startled him as he dismounted.

Jim Young rummaged in the spring wagon and came back with three cold biscuits and a chunk of fried meat. Will wolfed them down, their salty taste more welcome than cake to his palate.

Mel Young said, "They crowdin' you, Will?"

"Some," Will said through a mouthful of biscuit.

"They brought that hand of Garretson's in last night," Mel said dryly.

Jim Young's shape materialized beside him. "Your grub's on your saddle, Will.

Here's the shells. Rifle's in your scabbard."

Will took the shells and reached for his tobacco and then checked himself. False dawn was breaking and time was short.

"How long do you figure it will take?" Will asked, then.

Mel said, "This is new for us, Will. We can't rightly tell."

"Do a job, that's all," Will said. "Take the time you need." He paused. "How's Ike?"

"Good. He wanted to come with us."

Will smiled into the darkness. "And Miss Evarts?"

"She ain't so good at waitin', Will," Jim Young said, and Will had a fleeting picture of Celia, restless and impatient, but not despairing.

"She saw Kneen, did she?"

"That's right," Jim Young said.

Then everything was ready to go, and yet Will still lingered. These were the first friendly voices he had heard since Celia had left him at Cavanaugh's, and he found himself hungry for talk. Yet he had to leave.

The Youngs followed him over to his fresh horse Jim had saddled, and Will stepped in the saddle. He said then,

"Reckon you two could meet me on the old logging road tonight around that black shale?"

At their murmur of assent Will lifted the reins and repeated:

"Take your time and do a job. Give me ten minutes."

He vanished into the timber now, keeping east, and in a few minutes could see the edge of it. He dismounted, loosened the saddle, and tied his horse back deep in the timber. Then, taking his gun and the boxes of shells, he went over to the edge of the timber.

Straining his eyes now, he waited, and presently the shape of Bide's shack and the shed and corrals below came into focus. He was less than seventy-five yards from the buildings. Leisurely, now, he chose the spot which would afford him the best vantage point, picked his tree, broke open the boxes of shells, and then, everything ready, reached in his pocket for his tobacco.

He had rolled and lighted his smoke when the sound came. It was the steady, regular sound of a sledge hitting metal and came from the direction of the Springs upvalley. For perhaps five minutes he heard it, regular as the ticking of a clock, and then he saw the shack door open and a man step out into the yard, peering up the valley.

Will carefully put down his cigarette, raised his carbine, levered in a shell, and fired.

Even in the half-light he could see the spurt of dust kicked up at the very feet of the man. Without looking the man dived back into the shack. Will put two shots into the shack door and then bellied down beside the tree. He put his sights, which he was beginning to see better now, on the small window at the end of the shack and then pulled off and fired. The smack of the slug in the logs came on the heel of the report of his gun. He waited a moment, giving them time to heed his warning, and then he put two shots through the window. He moved his sights and put another shot into the door and then pushed fresh shells into his gun, watching.

The faint murmur of voices down there in the shack came to him. Suddenly there was a shot, and Will heard the thud of the bullet in the tree above him. He smiled a little and moved deeper behind the tree trunk, and then put two more shots through the window. He heard a loud, bitter cursing inside the shack now and speculated on the reason for it.

It was daylight now, and the steady sound of sledging up the valley had never left off.

Will settled himself comfortably and watched. Presently a rifle barrel poked out of the shack's broken window, and quickly he put a shot at it and it withdrew. Again he put a pair of shots into the door and then, out of some whim, raised his sights to the stovepipe. It took four shots to bring it down; it bent, broke, rolled down the sod roof, and boomed twice as it hit the ground and rolled to a stop.

Again he loaded his carbine, and this time he put the gun aside, waiting.

Nothing moved down there. Nobody offered to come out.

The sun was fully up now, and still the sledging went on up the valley.

Will settled down to wait, and he wondered if the men in the shack understood what was taking place over at the Springs. If Russ Schultz was there, he might, but Will doubted if the others would.

For more than three hours Will kept his vigil, sending an occasional shot into the door or the window, and all the time the sledging up the valley kept up.

Presently it ceased, and there was a long silence.

Then a soft, ground-shaking thud came to him, so quiet he could feel it more than he could hear it.

A few seconds afterward the door of the shack slammed open and a man lunged out. Will's carbine lifted to his shoulder, and then over his sights he saw who the man was. It was Sam Danfelser, and he was running heavily toward the shed by the corral, oblivious to Will up in the timber.

Will's rifle slacked off his shoulder and he called sharply, "Turn around, Sam."

Sam Danfelser might not have heard him for the attention he paid him. Will looked beyond Sam and saw a man standing in the doorway, watching this. Cursing softly, Will put a slug in the doorjamb inches from the man's head, and the man dodged back and slammed the door.

Will looked down at Sam now. He had made the safety of the shed. The high, vertical cedar poles of the corral hid from Will what was going on in there, and he watched, a faint excitement in him. He could keep Sam a prisoner in there just as effectively as in the shack, but he wanted to know what Sam was going to do. The sledging had not been resumed up the valley.

Will watched, and then Sam's voice, thick with angry arrogance, lifted into the morning.

"Will, I'm riding out of here!"

Will heard the corral gate dragging and then the sound of a horse running. And then Sam, leaning over the neck of his running horse, came into view from behind the shed, headed for the Springs.

For a moment Will could only stare, more amazed than angry. Sam Danfelser knew he wouldn't be shot in cold blood by Will and he was taking his own savage, arrogant advantage of it. Will's gun whipped to his shoulder, and he waited a moment, fighting down his anger. Then he held his breath and fired.

Sam's horse simply collapsed under him, and he was pitched out of the saddle over his horse's head. He landed on his side and turned completely over in the air and came down with an impact that stirred a faint rising of dust.

Will lifted his voice in anger now. "Get back in the shack, Sam!"

Sam Danfelser dragged himself to his knees and hung his head a moment, moving it from side to side as if to clear it. And then he came unsteadily to his feet and looked in Will's direction. Sam's horse lay utterly still before him.

Sam pulled his gun then and, half running, half walking toward Will, he began to shoot.

It was on the heel of his second shot that it came.

There was a dull, vibrating impact on the very air, and the ground itself seemed to shift. And then a raw, sliding rumble followed it, continuing for perhaps ten seconds.

Sam halted and turned toward the Springs, completely oblivious to Will in the timber. He stood rooted there, watching something upvalley.

Will knew by the sound of it that the Young boys had done a job. Russian Springs was buried under tons of rotten limestone. Oddly now, watching Sam, his promise to Celia ribboned through his mind. He was not going to give Sam a chance to kill him yet.

He rose and faded back into the timber,

and then he heard Sam's wild yell to the men in the shack.

"Come out and get him!"

Will reached his horse, cinched the saddle tight, and vaulted into it. He put him back into the timber, skirting behind the shack, and kept to its cover for a mile until it petered out at the end of the valley.

He was a good two miles out into the flats, headed for the Salt Hills, when he saw the first horseman boil out of the timber in pursuit, and behind him were five others. That first horseman, Will knew, would be Sam Danfelser.

He settled down now to flight. There were long hours of daylight before him and miles of open country. He would need luck this time. He swung south a little and nursed his advantage carefully. His horse was fresh, and Sam Danfelser was angry. With reasonable luck this meant he would have more than a two-mile advantage when he hit the Salt Hills this afternoon and could reach Boundary unmolested.

Chapter 20

Sam reached Boundary around ten, having ridden the heart out of Bide's horse by midafternoon. The others had left him behind, but Sam had no hope of them catching Will.

He put in at the Belle Fourche's tie rail and did not even bother to tie the horse. It was worthless to him, used up, and all he knew or cared was that the horse had first failed him and then brought him here at the slowest of walks.

Sam paused on the plank walk, looking over the few horses at the tie rail. It was too dark to see their brands, and Sam was too impatient to look. He tramped up the steps of the saloon with a heavy, angry impatience. Bide had called to him as he had ridden away from the shack in pursuit of Will that he would see him in town tonight. Only in late afternoon had Sam recalled this, and now there was a vast impatience upon him.

He shouldered into the barroom, a stocky, sullen-faced man whom sustained anger had turned surly and dangerous. He still carried the dust of his fall at the shack on his rough clothes. An elbow of his coat had been torn in the fall; sometime in the afternoon he had ripped off half the sleeve, exposing a forearm of calico shirt.

He came up to the bar, glancing hotly over the room. It was almost empty tonight. He nodded to Lowell Priest in conversation with the bartender and saw Joe Kneen playing solitaire by himself at one of the tables. A quiet poker game was going on at a rear table.

Sam said roughly to the bartender, overriding Priest's talk, "Bide's not in, is he?"

"In the back room," the bartender said.

Sam started back just as Bide came out of the back room, saw him, and started toward him. Sam wheeled and went back to the bar and waited for Bide to come up to him.

Bide, unlike Sam, was past the point where he could sustain anger. There was a kind of weary, bitter irritability about him that alternated with gloom.

He said, "You missed him."

"On that damned crowbait horse of yours, yes," Sam said angrily. Neither of them bothered to lower his voice, since they had accepted long since that nobody else besides themselves counted here. The time to be tactful or persuasive in public was past, and if they had even seen Kneen they did not show it.

Bide said bitterly, "He did a job, all right." Turning, he said sharply to the bartender, "Whisky, dammit."

He regarded Sam broodingly. "That rotten limestone broke and sluffed off in a fifty-foot circle. You can't even tell where it was."

The bartender put the bottle of whisky by Bide. Sam reached out, appropriated the single glass, poured himself a shot of liquor and drank it. The bartender gave Bide a glass, and he poured himself a drink. He looked at it sourly a moment, then pushed it away from him.

"I've had some time to think," he said in a dour voice, and he looked sharply at Sam. "I wonder, by Harry, if you have."

Sam didn't answer him.

"In another month, maybe less, we move

off that range. These potholes will be dry and our stuff will have to leg it back to Bandoleer for water."

Sam said grimly, "None of my stuff will leg it back."

Bide shook his head. "Without the Springs, those wells won't water a tenth of your stuff."

"Hatchet will," Sam said flatly.

Bide looked sharply at him.

Sam poured himself another drink and raised it to his lips. He didn't drink, however; he put down his glass and said flatly to Bide, "Will figured if he blew the Springs, come dry weather we'd have to fall back on our range, didn't he?"

"Won't we?"

"Not me, I don't move back. When I move off that dry strip I move toward Hatchet." He drank his whisky and slapped his glass sharply on the bar.

Bide considered this a moment, and then his glance shifted past Priest, who had heard all this, to Kneen. He said loudly, "Hear that, Joe?"

Kneen didn't even look up from his game. "I heard."

Bide said, "I'm movin', too, and I'm not

waitin' for dry weather, even if Sam is. I'm takin' what Hatchet range I want." The poker game in the rear ceased now as these men watched Kneen. He gathered his cards, stacked them nicely, and rose.

"I don't think you are, Bide. I don't think either of you are. You got too much sense, in the long run."

Bide laughed shortly, jeeringly.

Sam didn't even bother to turn and look at Kneen, who moved his chair slowly out of the way and came around the table and up to them at the bar. Bide's black eyes were contemptuous.

Kneen said placidly, "You've both forgot something that Will didn't, and I don't think you'll like to remember it."

Bide watched him closely, Sam with unshakable contempt. "All this stretch around Russian Springs and south is open range. If a man claimed it and could hold it, it was his," Kneen began.

"We'll hold it," Bide said grimly.

"But not west of that stretch, you won't. Because all the water west of Russian Springs on Hatchet is on patented land." He paused, watching Bide's face, and the expression of contempt there altered faintly.

Kneen went on with mild implacability. "That shack west of the seep was Phil's original homestead. South of his was Hempstead's and south of his was Tevis'. There was eleven of 'em altogether. They all sold out to Phil and moved out. That was when he was buyin' range, instead of takin' it."

Bide said dryly, "That so? What does it mean?"

"It means you don't move onto it," Kneen said gently.

"You'll stop us?" Bide baited him.

"Oh no," Kneen said. "That's when I call in a U.S. marshal."

He waited a moment for that information to take hold, then nodded and stepped past Bide. Bide stood motionless as he passed and then whirled, grabbing Kneen's arm and abruptly hauling him around.

"No marshal's comin' in here, Joe!" Bide said harshly.

"Not while you're all janglin' over open range, he ain't," Kneen said mildly. "When you move onto patented land that's a case for the law. I admit I'm helpless—so I call in the government."

Gently he disengaged Bide's hand and

said dryly, slowly, "When you move it had better be back on your own range, gentlemen."

He nodded and started toward the door. Halfway to it Sam Danfelser's flat, surly voice hauled him up.

"Oh, Kneen."

The sheriff turned, and Sam said with massive sarcasm, "I'm so scared of you I'm going to hunt up a crew tonight and move my cattle tomorrow—onto Hatchet."

Kneen watched him narrowly a moment and then murmured, "Your privilege," and walked to the swing doors. There he paused and slowly turned to look back at the bar. Sam had turned his back to him, but Bide was still watching him. Kneen said, "If you still think that way by nine tomorrow morning I send for the marshal."

Sam didn't let on that he had heard him, and Kneen went out.

There was silence then. Priest pushed away from the bar and went out, his thin, precise steps tapping sharply on the floor and then the steps and then the boardwalk.

Bide was watching Sam intently, chewing a corner of his lip. His eyes were bright and excited and probing, and he watched every movement of Sam's with peculiar intentness.

He was aware now that the poker game had ceased, its players watching them. The bartender was watching, too, and Bide had an uncomfortable feeling of urgency. Sam poured himself another drink and cupped the glass in his hand, staring at his own image in the bar mirror.

Bide's patience finally broke. He asked almost pleadingly, "What about this, Sam?"

"Bluff," Sam said contemptuously. He drank his whisky and pushed away from the bar. Reaching in his pocket, he pulled out a coin and slapped it on the bar in a gesture of finality that seemed to sum up his complete indifference.

"You really think so?' Bide asked anxiously.

Sam looked at him, a withering scorn in his arrogant face. "I meant what I told Kneen, Bide. I'm going to round up a crew and move my stuff onto Hatchet tomorrow."

He tramped out of the barroom, and Bide watched him go. For the first time he could remember, Bide wasn't sure of himself. He was pathetically in need of Sam's assurance—but he didn't know; he just didn't know.

Priest hurried downstreet, cutting across the road to have a last look into his dark store before he slept. The scene in the Belle Fourche had scared him a little, but he had gleaned one piece of information from it that made him forget his fright. An excitement stirred within him when he thought of it, for it was a passport to profit. Kneen had said that he didn't care how many fought over open range; it was only when they encroached on patented land that he would interfere. And Priest knew that Phil Evarts, in latter years, had not bought land but had taken it. And almost the last he had taken was that range abutting Garretson's.

It was clear to Priest now that if he and Red Courteen could hold their new range against Hatchet they had a comfortable and profitable start in the cattle business, with nothing to fear from the law.

Priest thought of this and congratulated himself. Courteen was taking the risks while he put up the money. And Courteen had proven himself a tough enough customer to handle Will Ballard.

Priest turned in at the gate of his house and was almost on the porch when he felt somebody beside him. He whirled in fright, and a voice spoke quietly. "It's time we had a talk, Priest. Go on in."

It was Will Ballard. A faint residue of fear tugged at Priest then, but he conquered it. Will Ballard wouldn't hurt the father of Lottie Priest.

He opened the door and struck a match, and Will said quietly, "The kitchen."

Priest went on through the house and lighted the lamp in the kitchen. The places were set for breakfast on the table, and that meant Lottie was in, he noted with some relief. He gestured to a chair and said genially, "Sit down, Will."

When Will made no move to accept his invitation Priest looked at him. In some unaccountable way Will's appearance had changed, Priest noted uneasily. His face seemed thinner, his eyes deeper set, and the dark wash of beard stubble on his cheeks gave him a tough, raffish look. To Priest he seemed even bigger than usual, but he dismissed this as nonsense.

"Those are all your cattle that Courteen's grazing just below Garretson's, aren't they?" Will asked.

Priest nodded. "Red's and mine. We got a bargain from Garretson and the Ridge ranchers. Why shouldn't we buy them?"

"That's the mixed herd Red took from

Hatchet, isn't it?"

"Yes."

"I just wanted to be sure," Will murmured. "How bad do you want to keep them, Priest?"

At this moment both of them heard a movement behind Will, and they looked around. Lottie, a blue wrapper around her and her hair braided loosely down her back, was standing in the doorway. Priest felt an odd comfort in her presence here, and he smiled and explained dryly, "A business talk, I think, Lottie."

Will and Lottie regarded each other quietly, and in Lottie's face a small hope seemed to fade. She looked searchingly at Will and saw in his face only a weariness and a polite stubbornness, nothing else.

"I'll go then," Lottie said, and she was turning when her father said, "No, stay a minute, Lottie."

Will looked quickly at him. Lottie hesitated in the doorway, and Will said, "Why not? It'll save you telling her, Priest."

"Save telling me what?" Lottie asked. She was surprised at the coldness and suspicion in her own voice.

Will said slowly, "I was just telling your

father to move his cattle off Hatchet grass."

Priest said gently, "I don't think we'll do that, Will. You see, Phil Evarts stole that range, like he stole everything else. We've got as much right to it as Hatchet."

"If you can keep it," Will amended.

"Why shouldn't he be able to keep it?" Lottie asked sharply.

Will glanced at her, quiet astonishment in his eyes. He hesitated and then said bluntly, "Because I've never seen him fight—not even over a dollar."

Lottie flushed faintly. "Let's get this straight. Are you threatening Dad, Will?"

"Why, yes," Will said blankly. "That's just what I'm doing."

Lottie was silent, and she glanced over at her father. A faint smile played about his thin mouth, and his eyes even seemed amused.

Lottie observed wickedly, "He doesn't seem to be afraid of you, Will. Isn't that strange?"

Will's answer was immediate, blunt. "No. He won't do the fighting. Courteen will."

Will looked at Priest now. "Are you moving?"

"You know what my stand is on this,"

Priest said smugly.

Will said contemptuously, "Even Red Courteen doesn't deserve you for a partner, Priest."

"Will!" Lottie said.

Will turned to look at her, his eyes blazing. "You don't seem to understand this—neither of you. I'm going to drive Courteen off that grass if it means shooting!"

"Like you shot Cavanaugh?" Lottie said hotly.

Will said grimly, "That's my plan," and looked at Priest.

"I don't think you can do it," Priest said smugly.

Will put on his Stetson and went over to the back door and unlocked it and stepped out, closing it quietly behind him. Lottie watched him go, her eyes bright with anger and surprise. They were still bright when she turned to her father. "He means that, Dad."

"I know he does." Priest looked at her, doubt and irritation in his face. Now that Will was gone without further talk, he felt his confidence evaporating. He put his hands in his pockets and took a turn around the kitchen, and when he looked up Lottie was watching him. He thought he could detect a faint accusation in her eyes.

"Red can take care of himself," he said sharply.

"Shouldn't he be warned, though?"

Priest just looked at her, indecision in his face.

"Anybody can slip up on a sleeping man and shoot him in the back," Lottie said scornfully. Her voice turned bitter as she added, "I wouldn't put it past Will to try that, either."

"You think I should warn Red? I can't get a man at this hour to ride out there."

"Go yourself," Lottie suggested quietly. "The store won't miss you for a day."

Priest gnawed on his lip, standing in the middle of the kitchen. The full impact of this was just reaching him, and he was frightened by the implications Lottie had suggested.

"I'll go," he said suddenly. "I'll hitch up the buggy now and go out there." He felt better immediately and he started for the door. Suddenly he paused and turned to Lottie and regarded her speculatively.

"This might be the chance Danfelser and Marriner are looking for," he suggested. "It might teach Will a lesson."

He and Lottie looked at each other a long moment, a bond of sympathy between them. Then Lottie said with cold hatred, "I think it might," and she did not notice how closely her voice resembled her father's.

"I've got to hurry," Priest said. "Do you think you could slip on a dress and go down to the hotel and find Marriner?"

"I think I could," Lottie said, her voice cold and angry.

It was only when she was dressed and out on the street that it came to her what this meant. She paused in the dark, taken back a little at the thought that she was putting the pack on the man she once thought she was going to marry.

But he's a murderer, she thought defiantly, and she went on.

The clerk at the hotel was not awake. Lottie looked at the register, found the number of Marriner's room, and went upstairs.

At the door of the room she paused, hearing the murmur of voices inside. She had her hand raised to knock, when again the doubt rose in her mind. She knocked, then, almost angrily.

Bide Marriner opened the door. Beyond him she could see Russ Schultz seated in the open window. Surprise was in Bide's swarthy face. He bowed gallantly and then was at a loss, he could not invite her into his room.

Lottie said breathlessly, "I just wanted to tell you, Mr. Marriner. Will Ballard just left town. He's going to raid Red Courteen's herd over by Garretson's tomorrow." She hesitated, seeing the excitement blaze in Bide's face. Then a discouraged look supplanted it, and Bide looked at Schultz in the window. "Any of the boys here?"

Schultz shook his head in negation, and Bide turned to Lottie. "We'll have to pass it up. I've got to be in town tomorrow and——" He paused, his eyes narrowing. "Say," he began softly, "I thought you were goin' to marry Will Ballard."

Lottie did not even try to face that; she fled.

Chapter 21

Bide saw the sun come up with only a few hours of restless sleep behind him. He had learned one thing in those wakeful hours of the night: He did not have the nerves of Sam Danfelser. For Sam had left town last night, confident that Kneen was bluffing. Bide had spent the better part of the night struggling to achieve that same confidence, and this morning he knew he had failed.

He left his room just as full daylight touched the street outside. The porter was mopping out the lobby as Bide came down. Bide ordered him to get the keys to the cigar case from the clerk and went outside into the fresh morning.

Teetering on the edge of the porch, he listened with annoyance to the sound of the birds in morning song, and in his mouth was the gray taste of gathering fear. The air was cool and smelled of the grass on the long reaches of the flats south of town, but Bide did not notice.

The porter came out with his handful of cigars, and Bide lighted one and came down the steps and turned downstreet. A pair of dogs trotted angling across the street and disappeared between two buildings on some business of their own, and afterward the street was empty.

Bide walked slowly, and in his mind was the knowledge that he must come to some decision. If Kneen called a U.S. marshal in here and backed up his investigation that was the end of his own ambitions. That was a conclusion he couldn't avoid, no matter what Sam Danfelser thought. Idly Bide traced the course of these happenings and keenly saw where he had failed. With Kneen on his side the scheme had been flawless. And he had lost Kneen by insisting on the trial of Ray Cavanaugh. If he hadn't been so quick, so sharp, so eager for the short cut, Kneen would be with him today.

His cigar tasted foully, and he threw it away and looked around him. He'd walked down as far as the livery barn.

Gloomily he turned in and tramped down its runway and paused by the corral in back.

There were a dozen horses in here, and somehow it soothed him to watch them. He saw his own horse there, the one that Sam had ridden yesterday, and he knew, without having to ride him, that Sam had run the heart out of him. Thought of Sam moved him into deeper gloom. How could Sam be so sure that Joe Kneen was bluffing? With a sudden shrewd insight he guessed that Kneen had come up on Sam's blind side; Sam never believed anybody meant what they said except himself. This thought was not comforting either, and Bide turned away from the corral.

The urgency of this seemed even more insistent to him as he sought the street again and turned up it. In the brief half-hour of his stroll part of the town had come awake. Time was inexorably passing.

The earliest men to rise—the hostlers and the saloon swampers—were at their work. Bide paused and watched a stack of empty beer barrels rise on the sidewalk in front of the Belle Fourche, and on a sudden reckless whim he decided on a drink.

He went into the Belle Fourche and found the bartender with his coat still on. Bide moodily had a whisky, and when it sat heavily on his stomach he had another. But there was no comfort in alcohol this morning; it seemed to drive his deep pessimism into every corner of his body.

He paid up and went out to the steps of the Belle Fourche and stood there, looking at the waking town, and he thought, *I'm up against somethin' that won't move. Joe Kneen means it.* He had a quick image of Phil Evarts laughing at him and he swore bitterly to himself.

Because there was no place else to go now, Bide went over to the hotel and crossed the lobby and entered the dining room. He ordered a big breakfast and surprised himself by eating it, wolfing it.

Russ Schultz came down while he was eating and took a chair opposite him, and they did not talk. Bide watched Schultz's face and saw the unease in it, noticed his lack of appetite. *He knows Kneen isn't bluffin' too*, he thought dismally, and then his appetite was gone.

He lighted another cigar and saw Joe Kneen enter the dining room. He studied Kneen now, seeing him anew, and what he saw was not reassuring. Kneen had a fighter's face; his pale eyes were marble-hard, and there was something uncompromising in his smallest movement.

After several minutes of watching him Bide throught wryly, contemptuously, *I'm gettin' spooked*, and he put down his cigar and rose and went over to Kneen's table.

"Morning, Bide," Kneen said.

Bide slipped into a chair and folded his arms on the table and said, "Joe, would it make you feel any different if I told you I'd been a damn bullhead?"

"Not any," Kneen said quietly.

With gloomy fascination Bide watched him sip his coffee. Then Bide spoke again and there was desperation in his voice. "But, Joe, everythin's the way we planned it. You're a good man. You'll be kept on."

"I know I'm a good man," Kneen said mildly. "It took me some time to find it out, though."

Despair crossed Bide's face. He rose and went out of the dining room. Fleetingly he glanced at the lobby clock and he experienced a solid shock. Eight-thirty, it said. Bide had a moment of panic then, and he stood there staring at the clock, unbelieving, and he was thinking, *Where's Sam? He's got to help me.*

He turned toward the stairs then and,

mounting them, he stepped aside to let a woman pass. It was Celia Evarts, and Bide looked at her and did not recognize her.

Up in his room he locked the door and went over to the mussed bed and sat on its edge.

This was the way the dream ended, then. What Phil Evarts had left in Will Ballard's hands had somehow become the symbol of a politician's stubbornness. Bib M would remain just another spread, tolerated by Hatchet. Bide rejected that instantly, for in his mind's eye he had seen it otherwise. He had seen Bib M with more land than Phil Evarts ever brought Hatchet; and he had seen Bib M not even tolerating Hatchet.

He rose now and went to the window and looked out at the street. He heard a knock on his door and knew it was Schultz and did not answer, and presently Schultz went away. Bide stood there, feeling time pass, his courage naked and at last sufficient.

He looked at his watch now and saw it was a quarter to nine. Turning, he crossed the room and unlocked the door and went downstairs. The clock here said ten minutes to nine.

Bide stepped out into the street and

strolled up it and turned east and at the end of the block was in sight of the station.

He walked slowly now, cutting across the road, aware only of the irritating clang in a blacksmith shop off to his right. He crossed the cinder apron at the rear of the station and came around to the platform and put his shoulder against the wall.

His senses were sharp now, and he listened and presently, above the blurred sound of the life of the town, he heard the distant crunch of cinders.

Pushing away from the wall, he started toward the semaphore in front of the telegrapher's window, and he was even with it when Joe Kneen rounded the corner of the station.

Joe's pace slowed a little and he looked keenly at Bide.

He stopped now, almost at the open door into the waiting room, and he said, "Changed your mind, Bide?"

"Don't go in there, Joe," Bide said softly.

Kneen laughed at him and went in. Bide hurried now. He took the six quick steps that would put him through the door and into the waiting room and then he hauled up, seeing Kneen at the ticket window.

"Joe!" he said sharply, urgently, and Kneen turned to him.

"Don't do it, Joe. Don't do it."

Kneen watched him a still second and then turned his head and said distinctly, "Earl, I want to send a telegram."

It broke inside Bide, then. He reached for his gun and pulled it up hurriedly and shot, and he saw Kneen slap both hands sharply on the counter as he was brushed sideways and fell to his knees.

Then he saw Kneen's gun come up and Bide hurried. He shot twice, and then he saw Joe's gun pointing at him, saw it fire.

Something hit him; he had no memory beyond that.

The agent, murmuring, "Lord God!" over and over, came out of his office and hurried around the corner and almost tripped over Kneen.

The sheriff was still kneeling, pressing both hands against his side, and one hand still held his gun.

Kneen said, "Get me up to my room," in a thin whisper, and Earl did not touch him. He ran through the door that opened onto the town side of the waiting room and he bawled, "Pedro! Pedro!"

Coming back, he stopped. In his haste he had not seen what was on the floor by the bench.

Bide Marriner lay flat on his back, slid partly under the bench, and the floor under him was stained darkly with more blood than the agent had ever seen.

Earl looked at him and then looked away, his mouth tasting salty. He didn't pause on his way back to Kneen, for Bide Marriner was dead.

Chapter 22

Priest had left his house close to ten o'clock, and by the time he had driven five miles from Boundary on the road north, he knew he had made a mistake. His team settled down into a walk from which he could not rouse them, and he knew then he had driven them too fast. They were a fat pair of bays whose only exercise was a Sunday drive, and he should have known better.

Pulling up, he climbed out of the buggy in the darkness and ran a hand over the flank of the near horse. It was sweating heavily, and he could hear the labored breathing of them both.

He stood there in the dark, feeling an exasperation that was tinged with bewilderment. What was he, a storekeeper, doing on a rider's errand, anyway? A sense of futility enveloped him, and he looked about him. The land was dark, meaningless to his town eyes, and he had only a rough idea of where he was.

His first discouragement ebbing, he took stock of the situation. The need for haste was still acute, but with only a pair of stable-fat buggy horses there was nothing he could do. In his own mind he was racing Will Ballard, and there was no time to waste.

He climbed into the buggy again and drove on, watching the road for a landmark. He found one in the next mile: the turnoff to Ed Niles's old place, which he recognized. He had delivered a stove out here one Sunday years ago, but he did not know whose place it was now.

Turning off, he drove the quarter mile to the homesteader's building and pulled up in the dark yard. There was not even a dog around, and Priest's heart sank. He called out, however, in the fashion of the country: "Hello, the house!" No answer. He sat there in the buggy, anxious and baffled, and then he repeated the call with no hope of an answer.

He heard a stirring inside the house now, and the door creaked open and a man's voice said surlily, "Tucker ain't here."

Priest had heard this voice recently, and

his mind raced in trying to remember it. He had it. "Danfelser!" he called shrilly. "Sam Danfelser!"

"Who is it?"

Priest was scrambling out of the buggy. Hurrying through the gate, he ripped his coat on a piece of wire, but he did not pause until he was on the porch.

"This is luck," Priest said exultantly, and then, disliking enthusiasm in anybody, including himself, added, "You haven't bought this place, have you?"

"Tucker works for me," Sam grunted surlily. "Why shouldn't I be here?"

Priest made out his big bulk in the doorway. He said without haste, "Will Ballard just left town. He's on his way to drive my cattle off that grass by Garretson's, and I wondered if you——"

Before he was finished speaking Sam Danfelser was in front of him and had his hand on Priest's arm. Sam was gently shaking him.

Priest poured out the story of Will's visit then, and Sam cut him short. He dodged back into the house, and lamplight bloomed.

Priest stood in the doorway, oblivious to the shoddy room, and finished his story while Sam pulled on his shirt and boots and strapped on his gun belt.

"Can I get a change of horses here?" Priest asked.

"There's mine and one of Tucker's in the corral," Sam said curtly. "Come ahead."

He did not hunt for a lantern but took the lamp and, shielding it with his hand against the breeze, tramped out to the corral.

There was the immediate problem then of a saddle for Priest. Sam settled that by giving him his own. He saddled one of Tucker's horses for Priest and then put the bridle on his own horse and led them both out into the night and blew out the light.

"Let me unhitch first," Priest said.

"Hell with that!" Sam said roughly. "We're riding. Now."

He vaulted on his horse, which he rode bareback, and waited for Priest to mount, and then they rode out, leaving the bays hitched to the buggy and standing in the darkness.

The remainder of the ride was a nightmare for Priest, who did not like saddle horses. They traveled steadily and eternally, rarely alternating a lope with the steady walk of their horses, and Sam was silent. He seemed able to feel his way in the night through this country, and Priest did not question his judgment once he had told him where the herd was located. Sometime close to daylight Sam called a halt. This was where Priest had said the herd would be, and it was senseless to look for them in the darkness.

Priest slacked out of the saddle and lay on the ground, blessedly resting. Sam was on his feet, and Priest could hear him pacing back and forth restlessly, waiting for dawn.

It had barely broken before they heard the distant bawling of cattle, and Sam was again on his horse. This time he did not wait for Priest, but rode off impatiently.

By full daybreak they had spotted the herd and the smoke from the breakfast fire near by.

Priest and Sam rode into camp and were greeted by Courteen and his men. Red looked curiously at Sam and extended the ancient invitation of the country.

"Light and eat, you two."

"Nobody's eating," Sam announced flatly. "I want that fire put out too. Now."

Courteen had a rough retort on his lips when Priest cut in with his news. Will

Ballard was on his way to move the herd, and they had ridden all night to warn them. The fire was instantly put out.

Sam cut in then, saying, "How many men you got, Red?"

"Six."

Sam grunted. "Break up camp then. I'm going to take a look here."

Sam rode out toward the cattle, and Courteen watched Priest dismount painfully. Red said resentfully, "What's he got to do with this?"

"Let him run it," Priest said wearily. "He's out to get Ballard. That's all that counts, isn't it?" When Red nodded Priest added, "Better break camp in a hurry, Red. Don't cross him."

There was little work to be done, and the tarps and bedrolls were speedily rolled and packed on the pack horses.

Sam returned then, dismounted, and came up to Priest and Red, who were watching him curiously. The six men of Red's crew kept in the background, taking turns drinking from the coffeepot which they had salvaged before the fire was put out.

Sam looked about him now, saw a bare

patch of soil a few feet away, and went over and knelt by it, scowling deeply.

Priest and Courteen followed him, and when they had stood silently beside him for some minutes Sam began to speak.

"Over there on the other side of the herd, about a half mile, is an arroyo. Did you see it, Red?" He made a long mark with his finger in the dirt. Red nodded.

"We're all going to hole up there—horses, men, everything. We'll leave two men in sight to ride herd. You got that?"

"Sure," Red said a little irritably.

Sam was oblivious to anything Red might say now. He stared at him with a kind of terrible concentration, as if he were daring him to misunderstand or disobey.

"I want the herd moved over close to that arroyo," Sam said in the same insistent voice. He drew again. "I want it held there close to it. I want your two riders to be between the herd and the arroyo when Will Ballard comes. That will make him come around close to the wash to talk to them." He paused. "I want you to give me the first shot at him," he said flatly. "Afterward you can do anything you want—but that's the way it'll be. Understand?"

"Sure, sure," Red said softly, and this time his reply was not irritable.

Red swiftly explained to his men. Leaving two of them on guard, Red, Sam, Priest, and the four others circled the herd, which was grazing placidly now, and sought the arroyo.

It was some fourteen feet deep, with steeply sloping sides. Both rims of it were fringed by buckbrush and chamiso.

Sam told off one man to lead the horses up the wash, and then he stationed the others along the rim for perhaps seventy-five yards so that they were completely hidden.

Afterward he settled down in the buckbrush close to the rim to wait. Priest, who was next to him, tiredly studied his face.

It was patient, almost in repose. Sam himself sat utterly still, his head cocked a little to pick up any sound above the murmurous pulling of grass of the cattle as they ate beyond the rim.

Priest watched him a moment and then found himself not wanting to watch. He fingered the tear in his coat now but did not see it.

The man's crazy, he thought, and he found it oddly frightening to discover this in the bright, silent sunrise.

Mel Young said, "He's got 'em bunched," and looked over at Will and Jim Young. The three of them had topped a small knoll a half mile from the herd and had watched it for some minutes.

Will said, "How many men do you make out riding herd?" And when they agreed on two he was silent a moment. The green, tawny flats here stretched out in an almost unbroken evenness for a few miles until they were broken by the upthrust of the Indigos' foothills. Will scanned them carefully and saw no other riders. The cottony tips of thunderheads were peeping over the vaulting peaks of the Indigos already, Will noted idly, and he marked a coming rain.

He straightened in his saddle then and reached for his sack of tobacco. "Let's watch a minute," he murmured.

He fashioned a cigarette and lighted it and then crossed his arms and leaned on the saddle horn, pulling his feet from the stirrups. A weariness sat on his shoulders like a leaden weight, and he shut his eyes for a moment. He had a deep iron longing for sleep that was getting harder to conquer each day, and he wondered thinly how long he could stick this out. How long had he been at it, anyway? He tried to count the days and could not; they were blurred together, night jumbled with day, and only a few images stood out to give them reality. One of them, oddly, was the picture of Celia at Cavanaugh's that night when they had planned. The other real thing was the presence of the Youngs, tough, patient, loyal. Now he recalled Ike's warning when he had taken on the two rawhiders as Hatchet hands and he smiled to himself. These two had more than taken Ike's place. Without them he and Celia would have been helpless. Tiredly, now, he wondered what Sam's and Bide's next move would be and if Kneen had given his warning yet. Now the smoke from his cigarette stung his nose, and his mind seemed to tell his hand to take the cigarette away, and yet he did not move.

Then he heard Jim Young's quiet whisper, "The big fella's asleep, Mel."

Will seemed to fight his way up to the surface of his weariness and he opened his eyes, hauling himself erect in the saddle. He glanced at Mel Young, and Mel said, "Nothin' more, Will."

Will had to concentrate a moment to understand what Mel was talking about, painstakingly searching in memory for what he had said last. It came to him then that they were scanning the country, looking for more of Red's men, and he was all right again then.

"Two of Red's men were never much trouble," he murmured, and he put his horse down onto the flats, and the Young boys fell in beside him.

Presently they approached the herd, and Will saw the two riders plainly on the other side of the cattle. They saw him and the Youngs and yet they made no move to approach them.

Will's attention narrowed now as he tried to understand this. Were the two of them counting on him and the Youngs splitting up to circle the herd, which was stretched out in a long line, and then picking them off separately?

Will said quietly, "Stick together," and then he reined up. "Where's Red?" he called.

The riders stared at him silently, and then one of them answered, "In town."

Will said, "Tell him he can get his cattle at Hatchet. We're driving 'em off."

Still the riders did not move, and Will decided abruptly to go to them. He put his horse forward now, aiming through the herd, and the outermost cattle on the edge of the herd that were watching him turned against the others and started to move into it. Other cattle, in turn, moved with them, until the herd began to move ahead of Will.

Then the shot came—flat, vicious, close. Will felt the whisper of air close to his ear, saw the puff of smoke from behind a low chamiso, and for the first time saw the arroyo.

He understood in one swift, savage moment that this arroyo held Red and his men and that he had walked into a trap.

He yanked his gun out and took a snap shot at one of the punchers who had turned his horse toward the arroyo and he yelled, "Stampede 'em!" to the Young boys. Already the cattle were moving away from them toward the arroyo, and Jim Young let out a whoop and pulled his gun.

Now the whole arroyo for fifty yards seemed to open up in concerted fire. The cattle on the arroyo edge of the herd turned away from it, but the mass of the herd was already moving against them, and the few could not buck the gathering momentum of the many. The Youngs, not needing explanations, had fanned out in opposite directions against the flank of the herd and were shooting over the heads of the panicking cattle.

Will sent another shot at the lone puncher, who, from his rearing horse, was shooting wildly into the oncoming herd. Will saw the horse go over, heard the man's wild yell above the bawling cattle, and then the rising thunder of the running herd seemed to drown all else. The second puncher had vanished into the arroyo.

Will raced to the side now, shooting over the cattle. On the far side the cattle that were trying to stem the tide were pawing wildly and rearing up over the heads of the others, but the herd still moved indomitably against them.

Will's gun clicked on empty now, and he rammed it in the waistband of his overalls and pulled out his rifle.

Through the dust he looked across the herd and saw a puncher scramble up the far side of the arroyo and light out across the flats. Will shot at him and missed and shot again and missed, and then he looked to the right and saw Jim Young bearing down on him, yelling wildly and shooting his gun over the heads of the stampeding cattle.

Will put his horse close to the cattle again now and again let his gun off into the moil of dust that was rising from the stampede. And then, as if the earth had opened up to swallow them, the cattle in front of him seemed to sink into the ground. Will yanked back on the reins, and his horse reared sideways and away.

He got one brief sickening look at the arroyo bottom. It was a struggling, boiling mass of downed, bawling, fighting cattle that were trampling each other underfoot in a wild attempt to scramble out the other side.

Will's glance shifted then to a still form at the bottom of this slope. A steer, both legs broken, was futilely trying to struggle to its feet, and each time it fell back on the crushed, broken form of Red Courteen. His red hair seemed oddly colorless against the deeper red around him.

Will turned away just as he picked up the distinct voice of someone shouting, "The horses. Get your horses!"

Will looked across to the flats beyond the arroyo. Many cattle had reached that side and were running, still in panic, toward the mountains. He picked out four men still on their feet dodging among them, and one of these men was Sam Danfelser. Beside him, clinging to him, was the slight form of Lowell Priest.

Will turned and saw Jim Young paused on the lip of the arroyo, staring unbelievingly down at the struggling cattle. Will looked the other way then, and something caught at his throat.

Mel Young's horse had halted, and was standing motionless, the dust settling around him. And slumped over his neck, face buried in the mane of the horse, was Mel Young.

Someone down the arroyo was still shooting, the shots regular as the ticking of a clock. Will pulled his horse around and went back to Mel and dismounted. Jim Young rode up beside him now and dismounted too. Whoever was shooting now saw them, for a spurt of dust kicked up at Will's feet.

Will said sharply, "Let's get him out of here."

He mounted, took the trailing reins of Mel's horse, and, leading the horse, headed back in the direction from which they had come only a few minutes before.

The bare knoll afforded them some protection. In its lee Will dismounted again. He and Jim both saw Mel's shattered shoulder. His shirt down to his waist was dark with blood. Will said, "Mel, do you hear me?"

Mel nodded but did not speak. Will looked at Jim and said, "If he gets off that horse he won't get on again."

Jim Young's glance shuttled back to the herd. They were scattered far and wide over the flats. Moving among them, however, was a horseman leading two horses.

Jim said soberly, "Danfelser's there. If he caught Mel he'd shoot him."

Will nodded. "Want to take the chance?"

Jim Young's face was white, scared, and sober. He asked simply, "What do you think, Will?"

"Let's hit for the nearest timber and then decide."

Will took the rope off his saddle and swiftly looped it around Mel's ankle. Then he ran it under the horse's belly to the other ankle and, after taking a turn around it, looped it over the saddle horn. It would keep Mel in the saddle.

He looked at Jim now and his eyes were dismal. "This'll be rough, kid."

"Go ahead," Jim said.

They mounted now, and Jim, leading

Mel's horse, pointed toward the distant island of timber to the east on the flats. They rode steadily, hard, not sparing their horses, and when, an hour later, they pulled into the stand of live oak, Will reined up. He put his horse over to Mel and said quietly, "How are you, Mel?"

Mel tried to straighten up, bracing his good hand against his horse's neck. When he looked up at him his face was gray and lined with pain.

"Just keep goin'," he whispered.

Will glanced at Jim. "If we're lucky we've got a half-hour's start on them, Jim."

He turned now and scanned the flats they had crossed, but the long stretch of it was empty. He took his bearings now. To the north the pine-black shoulders of Indian Ridge were close, and he knew if he could reach them that he could shake off pursuit. But it was time they needed. No man could endure the agony that fast travel would bring to Mel, and if they didn't travel fast Sam and the remainder of Red's men could corner them out on the flats, and that would be the finish.

Will glanced at Jim Young, who was watching him with a dismal soberness in his eyes. He had never guessed how much these two strayed, broke brothers depended on each other, and he knew Jim hadn't either until now. Will said slowly, "Jim, we split up. You got to go it alone."

Puzzlement crept into Jim Young's face, and Will went on: "Look at it this way. Who does Danfelser want?"

"You."

"Then if he sees our tracks split, two going the same way, the third lining out, which would he take?"

Jim answered slowly, "The single. He'd figure you'd decided you couldn't help and were dodgin' again." Will nodded, and Jim, understanding now, shook his head and said quietly, "You ride out, Will. I can take care of Mel."

"You pull 'em off me for a few hours, Jim. By that time we'll be holed up at Cavanaugh's and safe."

Again Jim shook his head. "No man can keep on the dodge and take care of a hurt man. It ain't your job, Will."

Will said gently, "That's the only way it can be. When you've pulled 'em off me you can hunt up Celia. Get some medicine and some grub from her and bring it to me. I can't do it myself, can I?"

"It ain't right, Will," Jim said stubbornly.

Will smiled. "We're wasting time."

Jim Young sighed. "All right."

They rode through the live oaks and out into the deep grass of the flats beyond. Here they parted, Will leading Mel Young's horse and turning north toward the safe hills flanking Indian Ridge. Jim Young watched them go and then, after waving once, lined out east. Will knew how thin this was, but he had not watched Sam Danfelser all these years for nothing. The working of Sam's mind was simple and direct, and Sam would follow the single track, reasoning that no hunted man would ever burden himself with a wounded partner. He would think that because he would not, in a similar position, burden himself.

Chapter 23

As Sam became more certain during the gray afternoon that Will was heading for Hatchet he made his plans. There were enough of them—Priest and two of Red's hands—to hold Will here while Bide and his crew were brought in. In the back of Sam's mind the picture of what would happen then was not clear. But the outcome was. If Will was fool enough to try to make Hatchet he was a dead man.

Sam's reverie was interrupted by Priest's weary, querulous voice saying, "Who's this coming?"

Sam looked up and saw a rider quartering toward them out of the bald hills behind Hatchet.

Sam watched the rider and presently answered, "One of Bide's men. We've had 'em watching Hatchet for a week."

As the man came closer Sam noted

curiously that he did not seem in any hurry. Sam looked about him, seeing the grass waving in the ground breeze that had sprung up since the sun went under. Rain was coming he could tell, and he looked again at the approaching rider, who was still in no hurry. When the rider was close Sam impatiently put his horse ahead of the others.

"Did he go on in?" Sam called as soon as he was within earshot.

The rider came over to him and reined up and said, "Who?"

"Ballard."

The puncher's face was suddenly alert. "When was this?"

"Just now, you fool!" Sam said angrily. "He rode right past you, unless you were asleep."

"Not Will Ballard," the puncher said flatly. "No sir. Not him."

"Did anybody?" Sam asked slowly.

"Sure. One of them towheaded brothers rode in a little while ago."

Sam stared at him, speechless. The first faint rumblings of thunder over in the Indigos came to him above the sound of Priest and the others pulling in beside him.

Sam didn't move, but he felt an unspeakable rage uncoiling within him. They had been following the wrong man all afternoon. Will, with the hurt brother, was already over in the Indian Ridge country.

A sick wrath was in Sam then, and without a word he yanked his horse around and rode away from the others. He heard Priest calling to him and did not stop.

Later he was roused by the drops of water on his hand, and he glanced at the sky. It was almost dark, and he looked around him with a kind of surprise. The black, aching rage in him was dulled now, and he had not been aware of the passage of time.

Reining up now, he thought of what to do. He must build this all over again, and this time with more care, more patience. Twice this day Will had slipped through his hands, but Will could make mistakes. Thinking of it now, Sam decided that Will had already made one. If he had a hurt man with him, that meant he'd have to hole up, and in time his hide-out could be found. It would take all his men and Bide's crew, but they would find him.

Sam put his horse toward Boundary now, patient again as the large, sparse drops of rain thickened and turned into the first full bursting of the storm.

Long after dark Sam rode into Boundary. The slicker which had been on the saddle of the horse he had chosen at the stampede was too tight and, putting it on, he had split it across the shoulders. He was wet and cold and bone-weary, and the sight of Boundary, its streets pooled glassily with the rain, did not cheer him.

He looked at the warm light of the Bell Fourche and rejected it. More than anything else he was hungry and, turning in at the tie rail in front of the Stockman's House, he tried to remember when he had eaten last and could not.

He stepped down into the mud and tied his horse, oblivious to the fact that he was leaving it out in the rain. He had swung under the tie rail and was mounting the steps of the hotel porch when he heard his name called sharply: "Sam! Sam!" He wheeled ponderously and saw a man bolt down the steps of the Belle Fourche, dodge under the tie rail, lose his footing, fall to one knee in the mud, and come up again, cursing. He recognized the voice of Russ Schultz, and a faint premonition tugged at him.

Russ splashed uncertainly across the street and ducked under the near tie rail and came up to him. His heavy face, turned up now into the rain-streaked light, was harried and anxious, and he said, "You heard?"

"What?"

"Kneen got Bide."

Sam accepted this, repeating it to himself, but he was thinking, *That leaves just me.* Oddly this news had no power to move him. Kneen wasn't bluffing, and Bide thought he was, and that was all there was to it. Sam's mind was almost placid, barren of regret; he was aware of his hunger and of a vast, gathering impatience.

When he did not speak Schultz gave him the account of the shoot-out. Hearing it, Sam had a fleeting impersonal admiration for both men, and that was all. Schultz had talked himself out, and there was nothing left to say.

Sam said then, "Where's Kneen?"

"In his room."

Sam made a move to go, and Schultz said quickly, "Be careful, Sam. Miss Evarts is there." Then, as if he had just thought of it, he added, "He wants to see you."

"Sure he does," Sam said mildly and

went in. Schultz followed him as far as the lobby and watched him climb the stairs and he was puzzled.

Kneen had been moved from his old room, and Sam had to come down again and ask where he was. He was directed to the second-floor-front suite.

Sam approached the suite and did not knock. He palmed the knob and stepped in and saw Celia sitting in a chair beside the table in front of the parlor's middle window.

She was dressed in black riding clothes, and Sam looked at her a moment, feeling nothing except the old, old impatience. Celia rose and said, "He's in here, Sam. Don't talk to him long," and started for the next room, and Sam wordlessly followed her.

He paused just inside the door and looked curiously at Kneen. The old man was flat out in bed, no pillow under his head, and when he turned his head to see who entered Sam saw his pale eyes were sick, pain-filled.

Sam tramped over to the bed and regarded Kneen a moment, his face unrelenting, unpitying. He said softly, "You only did half a job, Joe." Kneen wet his lips with his tongue and said in a fragile, toneless voice, "Stay off Hatchet, Sam. I'll warn you like I warned him."

Sam's smile was slow, musing. He found he had no business with Kneen after all, and he turned away and went out of the room. Celia had left Kneen's room and was standing in the middle of the parlor.

Sam paused, looking at her, his heavy face impassive, his eyes watchful. He was aware that his slicker was dripping water; he could hear the drops faintly touch the rug, and he looked at Celia as if she were someone he hardly knew.

He said mildly, "Are you happy now?"

Celia said, "Give up, Sam. It's over."

Sam's smile was slow, again musing, and he said, "No. No, I don't think so." He paused. "There's Will," he suggested gently. There was no expression in Celia's face except a kind of pity, which Sam did not see.

"Yes sir," he murmured, as if to himself, "there's Will." And he left her, closing the door behind him.

Downstairs in the lobby Schultz came up to him, and Sam went out the door and halted on the porch. Schultz followed him out, and Sam stood there, looking out at the rain blurring the reflected lights in the hundred small puddles of the street, feeling his impatience.

Schultz said, "What happened to Priest? He pulled in at the store and fell off his horse."

Sam didn't answer him, and they were quiet.

Schultz said presently then in a bitter, unguarded voice, "I wish he'd gone after Ballard like he had the chance."

Sam turned slowly and said, "Who?"

"Bide. She told him. She tried to send him out, but he was worried about Kneen. He could of missed him."

Sam said, "Who?"

"Bide. He——"

"Who told him?" Sam asked.

"Lottie Priest. She come and told him about Will last night, and he wouldn't go. He——"

"Shut up," Sam said gently. He was looking at Schultz, not really looking at him either. His slow, methodical mind considered this, first with a tentative, faintly skeptical speculation, and then with curiosity, and then, much later, with a rising conviction.

He said, "Why, yes," as if in answer to some question Schultz had asked him, and he went down the steps and turned upstreet, hurrying now.

Schultz watched him go, and he was puzzled and faintly uneasy. Sometimes he didn't understand Danfelser, and this was one of the times. Schultz went back into the empty lobby and, after a turn through it, sank into a chair. He did not know what to do with himself. There was a man lying dead on a table in the back room of Johnson's Hardware Store, and because of this Schultz didn't know what to do with himself. His was a bought loyalty, and it was on the market again, with no immediate taker. Sam had surprised him by not wanting it, and Schultz, a simple man, was at a loss. He heard the lobby door open and looked over and saw Jim Young, his slicker dripping rain, tramp through the lobby and mount the stairs, and Schultz speculated idly and with complete neutrality on his business.

He was still speculating on it when Jim Young and Celia Evarts came downstairs. Celia had on a man's slicker and Stetson and she was in a hurry. They both went out, and Schultz stared idly at the doors. He yawned and then, curiosity stirring, he rose and went out onto the porch. Looking upstreet and then down, he could not see them and he forgot them.

It came to him then, watching the steady slanting rain, that he was through here. Across the street at the Belle Fourche there were men waiting for their orders, and he did not know what to tell them because nobody had told him.

A feeling of bafflement, almost resentment, welled up in him at the thought. Danfelser couldn't use him, and Bide was dead, and he was through.

He wandered back into the hotel and slacked into a chair and presently slept. He was awakened by someone shaking him roughly. Opening his eyes, he looked into Sam Danfelser's face. Something had happened, Schultz knew; he could tell it by the faint, brash glee in Sam's eyes as he stood looking down at him.

Sam said, "I know where Will is." Schultz came out of his chair. He had a purpose now; he had orders.

"Everybody's over at the Belle Fourche. Give me a minute," he said.

"No," Sam said. There was a half-smile on his lips. "I just want you along." He started for the door now, Schultz at his elbow, and said mildly, "Why didn't I think of her before?"

Chapter 24

Celia stood in the archway of the livery barn while Jim Young saddled her horse and brought him to her.

She saw the fear and the worry in his face as he came up beside her and handed her the reins, and she said, "Will's with him, Jim. We'll do everything we can."

"I know," Jim said quietly. He gave her a lift into the saddle and handed her the saddlebag filled with medicine that the doctor had given them, and she took the reins. "You don't blame the doctor, do you, Jim? Kneen had first call on him."

"I don't blame him," Jim said tonelessly.

Celia said quietly, somberly, "When you bring him out, Jim, be careful. Be awful careful nobody's following."

Jim nodded and said gratefully, "Thanks, Miss Evarts," and saw her ride out into the night and vanish.

Celia watched the road behind her, and she was certain she was not followed. She tightened the slicker strap around her throat and settled down to the long ride, trying to summon the patience to make this bearable. She would never forget the look on Jim Young's face as he stepped into the parlor back in the hotel. She saw that tight, somber look on his young face and thought instantly, *They got Will,* and the relief she felt when she learned it was Mel who was hurt made her feel a kind of shame now.

But not much shame, for how else should she feel? Bide's death this morning had been ugly enough, but it had resolved the bitter fight, freeing Will and Hatchet with him. All day long she had sat beside Joe Kneen, blessing his courage, trying in the only way she could to thank him for herself and Will. But all during the day, too, she had wondered with a kind of dread what Sam would do with Bide dead. Tonight she had her answer. Not in words, perhaps, but in Sam's stubborn, taciturn face, in his insane, implacable hatred for Will.

Jim Young's news had brought a wild relief, but it was short-lived when she remembered Sam. For she remembered another thing, too, a few words that were graven in memory. Will had spoken them. *I promise you one thing,* he had said. *Sam won't get a chance to kill me until Hatchet is on its feet again.* And now Hatchet was free, and Will was left to carry out what was implied in his promise. He wouldn't dodge Sam now; he would hunt him out.

So if she was honest with herself, she would admit that the medicine for Mel Young was only an excuse for her riding out in this rain to Cavanaugh's. She had come to see Will, not only to tell him, to warn him of Sam, but because she needed him, had to see him. And being honest, she admitted it to herself and, having done so, felt better.

The rain seemed to slacken when she reached the timber above the foothills, but she knew that was because of the trees. She knew these trails intimately and she rode with a reckless haste that she could not explain. The dripping timber around her smelled of cold pitch and rotting needles, and as she climbed higher and deeper into Indian Ridge she could hear water runneling along the center of the trail. Long hours after midnight she put her horse down the trail into Ray Cavanaugh's tight little valley and presently came onto the valley floor and past the corral.

The shack was dark, and as Celia approached it, passing the well, she called softly, "Will! Will!" wondering if he had not reached here yet.

The answer was immediate. "Celia."

She dismounted, forgetting her horse, and ran for the porch, and Will stepped out in the rain to meet her. Celia had herself in hand now, and she said, "How is he, Will?"

"Sleeping," Will said. "Come and look."

Inside the shack Will struck a match and touched it to a stub candle.

Celia covertly, almost hungrily, watched him as the flame crept fully alight. His face looked tired and drawn, and his eyes were sunken deep in their sockets. He glanced at her, surprising her watching him, and his face was less grave and he smiled.

Together, then, they tiptoed over to the bunk. It was still on the floor, and Mel Young was covered by its dirty blankets. He lay on his back, breathing the deep, slow breaths of exhaustion. His face was flushed, but he was quiet. His shoulder was hidden by bandages of torn shirt, and Celia noted with relief that they were not stained with blood.

She glanced at Will, and he was eyeing her quizzically.

"Shouldn't we let him sleep?" Celia said.

Will nodded, and Celia turned away. Will followed her out onto the porch and closed the door behind him. They sat down, side by side, backs against the log wall.

I can say it now, she thought and said, "Bide is dead, Will. Joe killed him." She told him of the fight at the station and she watched his face, unable to see it in the darkness. His presence was close, and what she told him seemed somehow less dreadful because of it. She told him of Kneen, that the doctor had thought him out of danger if he got through the night, which he seemed to be doing, and all the while Will said nothing. Even when she finished telling him he did not speak.

Presently she said, "What are you thinking, Will?"

"Of Kneen," he answered slowly, and then, much later, he added, "Of Sam, too, I reckon."

"He came into Kneen's room," Celia said quietly. "He was like a man walking in his sleep with his eyes open." She reached out and touched him and said miserably,. "Will, all he wants is to get you, to kill you."

"He can try."

"He *will* try."

"All right," Will said calmly. "I'm through dodging him, though."

"I know. I didn't mean that. Only when you ride into Boundary, Will, he'll——"

Celia felt Will's hand laid gently across her mouth, and then it fell away, and cold, stark fear was in her. She heard the whisper of cloth as he rose, and she rose, too, beside him. She held her breath, straining every nerve to hear as they both listened. It came to her then—the soft squishing of a horse approaching from behind the house.

She heard something else, too, now. It was the whisper of Will's gun sight raking the worn leather of his holster as he lifted his gun out.

She felt his arm laid across her, brushing her against the door, and she whispered wildly, "Take my horse, Will, and get out!"

"Go inside," Will said gently, and he moved away from her toward the end of the porch.

Celia knew a dismal fear then. The rider approaching couldn't be Jim Young or he would have sung out. It was Sam, for only Sam would hunt him now. And Will was cornered in the dark. She thought, *Any way but this*, and she heard her horse whicker nervously.

Celia knew what she would do then. She stepped softly off the porch into the rain, moved quietly toward her horse. Will would be watching the corner of the house, and he wouldn't know until too late.

When she reached her horse she vaulted into the saddle and savagely roweled him around toward the corrals. The splash he made in turning was loud in the night, and above it Celia heard the sound of a galloping horse.

She heard, too, Will's wild cry, "Celia!"

Will yelled it into the night and lunged off the porch into the rain, and a rider passed him, galloping headlong.

Will shot blindly, running, and the horse vanished into the darkness, and he hauled up in the rain, a wild despair in him. She had drawn Sam off, and he would kill her, not even knowing whom he was shooting.

And then he heard a movement, faint but unmistakable, behind him, and he wheeled in the slanting rain, alert.

"You're there, Will. Answer me."

It was Sam Danfelser's voice, and it came from the corner of the house. A cold and wicked joy curled somewhere inside Will and he said, "I'm here, Sam," and started for him, running. He heard Sam running, too, and knew it would be toward him and that Sam would shoot as soon as he could see him, just as he himself would shoot.

He ran toward the sound of Sam's heavy splashing feet and then suddenly, only feet in front of him, the night exploded in a bright, blazing flash. Will lunged for that flash, his gun in front of him, and he felt it prod into something and he shot. The shot was muffled, and then Sam's body smashed into him, a long, bubbling groan rising into the night, and Will lost his footing and fell in the mud.

He came up and heard a slow, strangling burble and he lunged again for it and tripped over something on the ground and slipped and sprawled across Sam's body. It lay face down in the mud, arms above the head, and as Will crawled back to it he heard the wet, rattling sound of a man's last choking breath.

Will rose and stepped over him and ran

blindly toward the corrals. He heard a horse slipping down the trail and then someone called, "Sam?"

Will shot. A bawl rode into the night. "Will! Will! It's me! She's all right. She's all right, I tell you!"

Will, still running toward him, heard Celia call from somewhere ahead of him up the trail: "Will! Will!" and he halted, panting, lifting his face toward the sound of that voice. He could tell, he knew she was all right, and there was an unspeakable gladness in him.

Schultz's horse moved past him, skirting him widely in the darkness, and Schultz called out then, "I quit, Will. I've quit. You hear me?" Will didn't answer, and Schultz, not waiting for an answer fled. Will was running blindly toward the trail, a nameless urgency in him, a haste to see her and feel her and speak to her. He saw her horse then and he hauled up, and he saw her step down and come to him. He held her, wordless, in the steady rain.

ABOUT THE AUTHOR

Luke Short, whose real name was Frederick D. Glidden, was born in Illinois in 1907 and died in 1975. He wrote nearly fifty books about the West and was winner of the special Western Heritage Trustee Award. Before devoting himself to writing westerns, he was a trapper in the Canadian Subarctic, worked as an assistant to an archeologist and was a newsman. Luke Short believed an author could write best about the places he knows most intimately, so he usually located his westerns on familiar ground. He lived with his wife in Aspen, Colorado.